CW00405700

BILLIONAIRE'S BABY SECRET

A BILLION SCANDALS SERIES

L.A. PEPPER

© Copyright 2019 - All rights reserved.

It is not legal to reproduce, duplicate, or transmit any part of this document in either electronic means or in printed format. Recording of this publication is strictly prohibited and any storage of this document is not allowed unless with written permission from the publisher except for the use of brief quotations in a book review.

This book is a work of fiction. Any resemblance to persons, living or dead, or places, events or locations is purely coincidental.

ABOUT THE AUTHOR

Like you, Leanne loves contemporary romance stories and is an avid reader. When LA is not writing the next Bad Boy Billionaire contemporary romance novel, she enjoys drinking a glass of Chianti, eating raclette with her girlfriends, participating in spin classes, and watching the sunrise every morning.

Leanne lives in beautiful Canada with her husband and kids.

She would love to connect with you! Check out her author page below.

https://www.amazon.com/LA-Pepper/e/B07QS4RJY6?ref_=dbs_p_ebk_r00_abau_000000

CHAPTER ONE: APRIL

"*C*ongratulations, mom," I said, feeling the words choke in my throat. "You look beautiful. I wish you and Joe all the best."

My mom, Barbara Hamilton-- no sorry, Barbara Gardiner now, since my dad was a mere six months dead, did look beautiful. Her perfectly highlighted platinum hair was cropped into a chic bob, and she wore a blue gown, not white for her wedding, because it was her best color and it set off her platinum blonde hair. She glowed. She looked happy. She'd never looked that happy with my dad. I ground my teeth together, knowing my smile probably looked feral.

"Oh, April." She tilted her head at me, astutely doubting my well wishes. Six months. That was all she had waited for. I missed my dad every day. I was still grieving and she'd just moved on. And I was having a hard time not being angry at her.

Without my dad between us, it was just us, at odds. Well, us and her new husband, Joe. Joe was tall and handsome, his blond extroversion clearly something she'd missed with my more dark and serious dad. Without him, my mothers' sharpness struck angry sparks against my stubborn intensity. Of course she didn't mention my dad. She'd never bring up the scandal of her quick remarriage. She'd just pretend it wasn't there and find something to pick at me about. Deflect, deflect, deflect.

"Did you have to bring the lesbian as your date to the wedding?" she whispered, grabbing me by the elbow and pulling me close so no one else could hear. "I know experimenting in college is a thing and I can understand that…"

"Mom--" I tried to stop her. Mona and I weren't dating. She was my emotional support friend because I couldn't handle how soon after my dad's death my mom had fallen deliriously in love. It felt like a betrayal, and I didn't particularly want to explore the feelings or my family's past.

"...But you know you have to find a man and settle down with him. Maybe you'll meet him in law school."

"Mom, I'm not going to--"

"Please, April, not at my wedding." People were looking at us. That's what she got for having such a small wedding. They all knew how disappointing her rebellious daughter was. "If your grandmother finds out about your... girlfriend, she could disinherit you. Is that what you want? She's from a different generation, you know. She's not as open minded as I am about lesbians."

I laughed out loud, wondering if it seemed like a happy laugh to the observers. Joe looked over at the sound. So did his daughter, Elisabeth, one of my best friends, a trio we were, Me, Elisabeth and Mona. She raised an eyebrow at me-- a warning. I was not allowed to mess up the wedding. I raised my eyebrow back at her, then turned back to my mom. Obstinate.

Open minded was she? I wished I was gay because Mona would have been a catch, my half black, bisexual, hippie best friend was one of the best people I'd ever known. But I didn't want to tell my mom that. I didn't want to let her off the hook. Besides, fighting with her over my best friend's sexual orientation was so much less painful than thinking about her betrayal of my dad.

"Mona is a bisexual, mom, not a lesbian. And she's here because I love her." My mom gasped. She hated scandal worse than anything. "She's staying with me for the summer and then we're thinking about opening up a yoga studio." I wasn't lying, but it sure sounded less platonic in context. I grinned. "You're going to have to make do with Jack as a perfect child. He's the one who met his fiancee at Harvard Law. You can give up on me now."

"April!"

From out of nowhere-- okay not from out of nowhere, my voice had clearly gotten too loud for circumspection-- two lovely ladies swooped in on me and took ahold of my elbows from either side.

"Lovely wedding, Mrs Gardiner. I've never seen such a meaningful ceremony," Mona said from my right, her short fingernails digging into my bare arm.

"I'm so happy to welcome you into the family, Barbara. My dad is so happy." I didn't even have to look at Elisabeth to know she was turning her stunning golden girl smile on my mom, pacifying her. Elisabeth was very effective that way. "Mind if we take April for a little college reunion?"

"We just graduated in June, hardly long enough for a reunion," I said. Clearly they were saving me. Or saving my mom. And I was being ungrateful.

"And we haven't all been together since then," Mona's dry voice gave away nothing, but I knew it was an excuse. She was running interference.

Joe came up and put an arm around my mom's shoulders. He was running interference from the other end. "Look at all my beautiful girls," he said. I watched my mom's face come alive. The tenseness she got when I was around just faded away. Tears came to my eyes. I was happy for her. I was. "Do you ladies mind if I steal my wife away?"

I shook my head and watched them go, left with my girls, closing ranks around me. "You promised, April. You said you'd be nice for the wedding." Elisabeth gave me a look, her golden blonde curls cascading down her shoulders. She always got her way.

"Leave her alone," Mona snapped. Tall and slender, she looked down on both of us, her wild curly brown hair pinned with tiny flowers and her light brown skin glowing in the sun. She was also a force of nature. "She's sad about her dad dying. She has a right." Sometimes I felt caught between the two of them. Luckily, they were both on my side.

Elisabeth sighed. "You're right. It sucks. But we're also not going to let your sadness ruin our parents' wedding, right?"

"I don't want to ruin the wedding, but I'm just so…"

"Don't worry." Elisabeth put her arm around my shoulder and led me to the bar. "We're going to distract you."

"Oh yeah? How?"

"Hot guy watching."

"Hey, bisexual here." Mona, happy again, had tucked her arm in mine as we strolled across the backyard to the bar. "Equal opportunity hot guy and girl watching, please."

Elisabeth nodded. "Gotcha. Hot guy and girl watching. That is always fun. What else is there to do at a wedding? Except hooking up."

"That's a great idea Lissie, but I'm related to all the guys here." A gross thought.

Elisabeth held a finger up. "Not true. There's the hot bartender." They cast their eyes, as one, over to the bartender. He had a scruffy beard and long hair tied back into a bun, and they could just see the edge of tattoos peeking out from under his long sleeved dress shirt.

"Very hot," I agreed. And he was, but he frankly looked too dangerous to me. For all I rebelled against my mothers ridiculous social expectations I was not an actual bad girl. Then I looked at Elisabeth who was practically salivating over him. "But I think you might have called dibs on him."

"What?" she asked, blinking at me in surprise. "No, no. You're the one who needs a distraction. I bet he could distract all. Night. Long."

I had to laugh, and hugged her arm. "It's your parent's wedding too. You get to have a distraction. It's okay you can call dibs."

The three of us laughed. "Okay I have dibs on the hot bartender, let's go get a drink and find out how distracting he can be in public."

We started forward but Mona pulled us back. "Oh, ugh. No. Your brother just sat down at the bar, April. Oh my god, did you know he thinks climate change is a conspiracy theory put out by the radical left?" Mona brown eyes lit with an internal fire behind her glasses. I thought she might explode. "I can't go over there. I think your mother might think the murder of her son at her wedding is a scandal. I'm here to prevent drama, not cause it."

Jack was indeed sitting at the bar being perfect with his perfect blonde fiancee, chatting with the bartender. I didn't want to go over there either. He could be a perfect ass and I didn't feel like dealing with him today, always so smug and superior. "I'm surprised you haven't murdered him already. For a vegetarian, you are incredibly blood thirsty."

Mona snarled, showing her delicate canines. "I only go for the monsters," she said.

Elisabeth laughed and spun them all, arms still linked, so that their backs were to the bar, looking over the expansive yard, and the path beyond, over the dunes to the beach. The yard was lovely. The caterer and party planner had done an excellent job. My whole family was happy, and the wedding party was my whole family. "We'll put a pin in the bar. Let's survey the other candidates."

"You don't have to Lissie. It's pointless. This wedding is too small and it's all family." I pointed with my chin at the two handsome men who had already stripped off their ties and were flirting with the waitresses as they were passing out appetizers. "Dave and Paul. Cousins, and frankly they're trouble all the way through anyway, even if they weren't related." I thumbed over my shoulder at the bar. "My brother Jack and his fiancee and the only hot single guy here who you have dibs on." I turned us to the side to see where my grandma had set up court on a lounge chair. "That handsome fellow with my grandma is Matthew. He grew up next door to me, so not related but, too young, and he's like a little brother. In fact, I like him better than my own brother, but no. Not an option." My mom and Lissie's dad danced by us, lost in each other. I rolled my eyes. And pointed to the last guests, sitting at a table, the best man and matron of honor. "And there's my aunt and Mr. Beaumont. See? Not one single distracting prospect."

"Well--" Lissie stopped me. "Well, wait a minute. Why is Beau not a distracting prospect?"

He actually did look very nice but I nearly choked. "You call him Beau?"

She smiled that smile that made me worried she had a plan. "He told me to. You call him Mr. Beaumont?"

"I've known him since I was a kid. He was my father's best friend. He's obviously not a prospect."

Mona twirled a lock of hair around her finger and cocked her head, looking at Beau-- Mr Beaumont. "That is a handsome man."

"Not you too."

"What? I thought we were looking for distracting prospects. That man is hot. He asked me to call him Beau, too. You're the only one who calls him Mr. Beaumont."

A shiver went down her spine. "This is inappropriate. He was my father's best friend. He's way too old for me."

Both girls shrugged. "Age is just a number," Mona said philosophically. "What matters is if your souls connect."

"Screw souls. We want their happy parts to connect." They both cracked up at Lissie's raunchy joke. I felt a blush heat my cheeks. "You're an adult. He's an adult. You're not related. And he is a silver fox, April."

"He is definitely a silver fox." Great. My best friends were in agreement. That made things dangerous for me. Whenever they plotted together, they were sure to reach their aim.

"You're both crazy," I said, but surreptitiously glanced over to where he was sitting with my aunt. It was true he was handsome, and he did look rather young, but for his hair. Bright silver. He'd always been like that as long as I could remember. And he didn't seem to have aged a bit. In fact, he seemed rather ageless. Mona and Elisabeth kept on chattering, but I watched Mr Beaumont-- Beau. It felt weird to even think of the casual name. He smiled at my aunt and the warmth in it took my breath away. He had dimples, too. I had never noticed that. I couldn't tell from this distance, but I knew he had stunning eyes, a light, bright green with dark eye lashes and eyebrows. They had always fascinated me.

He'd taken off his suit jacket on this warm early September day, and rolled up his sleeves. He had great arms. Strong and muscled. I imagined they would feel wonderful wrapped around me.

"Oh thank goodness," Mona breathed. "Jackass is done with the bar. We can get a drink."

I burst out laughing. "By Jackass, do you mean my brother Jack?"

Mona used one finger to push her glasses back up the delicate slope of her nose. "You bet I do," she grinned.

The three of us giggled our way over to the hot bartender where Elisabeth proceeded to take charge and order us gin and tonics and find out the hot bartender's name was Duke, which was perfect for his bad boy look. It was endlessly amusing to watch them flirt and to dip in and out of the conversation... but I couldn't take my eyes off the silver fox only a few yards away.

CHAPTER TWO: CHARLES

"*W*hy are you drinking alone, Beau?"

Donna, the matron of honor, sat down beside me and I smiled up at her. She was a lovely lady. I poured a glass of champagne and slid it along the table towards her. "I'm not drinking alone anymore, am I?'

She scoffed but took the glass. "Foolish man. You know I don't count."

"I beg your pardon, why is that?" She seemed immune to the smile that had charmed and disarmed many a woman before her.

"Because this is a wedding. And weddings are about love. You should be sitting with some pretty girl and making her smile."

"Are you offering, Donna?"

She rolled her eyes. Definitely immune. "You're a flatterer, but no. I was talking about those girls over there."

She pointed to the trio I'd been trying not to watch all night. Each girl was more beautiful than the next. The tall and svelte, light skinned black girl, Mona. The powerhouse blonde, Elisabeth-- Joe's daughter-- who was not someone to take lightly. And the worst one of all. April Hamilton. The daughter of my dead best friend. I'd watched her grow up, from a distance, of course. I'd always been busy with work and life and for some reason, I hadn't been paying attention because the last time I'd seen her she'd been a gawky kid, and now? I cleared my throat. "I'm too old for them."

"You're too old for yourself, Beau." Donna smiled wryly at me, as if her decade or so more of life had made her wiser. Perhaps it did.

"That doesn't even make sense."

"When you moved into the neighborhood, you were scandalously young, you and that wife of yours. We all knew you just married her because she was pregnant. And you just settled right in being the dad and husband and you never had a chance to even be one of these kids." She pointed at David and Paul, her twin sons, mid twenties at this point, who had always been trouble. Right now they were hitting on the two waitresses. Donna watched them and shook her head.

He needed something stronger than champagne, but that would mean he'd have to get up and go to the bar, where right now April and her friends were congregating. "Is there a point to this conversation?"

"Yes there's a point, Beau, don't give up on life. You're allowed to be happy. You gave everything to your marriage and now it's done, but that doesn't mean you have to be. You're allowed to find love."

"Maybe I don't believe in love."

"You are such a liar. You're the one who introduced my sister to her new husband and I've never seen two people more in love. You did that. And I know you thought they'd be good together. You believed in them. And I think you want that for yourself."

"So what if I do? That doesn't mean I'm going to find love tonight."

"It doesn't mean you won't. Why not take a chance?"

He shook his head no, and took another drink.

"Okay, I tried to be cupid." she sighed. "Just in case, let me put in a bid for my niece. I actually think you'd be good together. She's a lot more serious than most people think she is, certainly more than my sister does, who can't get past that she wants to be a painter. Nonsense, really. Nothing wrong with a girl who has an inner life, don't you think, Beau?"

I didn't answer. I also hadn't known April wanted to be an artist. I didn't know why, but the thought delighted me. I'd love to see her work.

Donna smiled again, then stood. "I'm going to go see if I can talk to the caterer and maybe get her recipe for those shrimp puffs." I watched her go, but my gaze caught on the trio again. And this time, I didn't even see the others. The only girl I saw was April. She wore a pale green off the shoulder dress that floated around her lithe body. With her long dark hair up in a loose bun, curling tendrils fell to caress the skin left bare by her dress. The graceful line of her collarbone entranced me. I laughed at myself and poured another glass of champagne. I'd better not drink too much, I had to make sure I didn't do the unwise things April's clavicles made me want to do.

CHAPTER THREE: APRIL

*N*ight was falling. The air was sweet and I could hear the surf just over the dunes. Dinner had ended long ago, and I was enjoying just being out under the starry East Hampton sky. It was early September and the last gasp of summer. It would probably start getting cold soon. I loved the beach house and used to come out here all the time in the off season, as well as spending my summers here, but knowing that my mom and Joe were happily in love newlyweds, I didn't want to intrude. I felt like an awful daughter that their happiness made me sad.

Everyone was busy. My mom and Joe were fantastically enraptured with each other. My brother Jack was arguing with Mona about the environment while grandmother was telling his fiancee stories of her scandalous days as a young girl. My cousins, Dave and Paul were, apparently playing some sort of ball game on the beach in the dark, with Matthew, and I hoped they weren't corrupting him, but I could hear them laughing along with the occasional high pitched giggles of some girls. I didn't know where they found girls to flirt with at this wedding. Maybe those waitresses. Grandmother's driver was already there, helping her up so she could retire early. She said the night made her yearn for more civilized comforts, like a blanket pillows and a martini.

Elisabeth was still at the bar, talking to Duke. I didn't want to interrupt, but…

I took my cell phone out of my little purse and sent her a text.

Me: I'm bored.

I watched her pick up her phone and read it. She glanced over at me before speaking quickly to Duke and then texting back.

Lissie: I'm halfway to getting the hot bartender to do me in the outdoor shower on his next break so I suggest you find something to distract yourself with.

I let out a breath of frustration. Of course she was

achieving her goal. She never let anything stop her. Another text dinged.

Lissie: … or someONE.

I stuffed my phone back in my purse without responding. Elisabeth laughed and turned back to Duke, leaning over the bar so he could see her ample cleavage. She was absolutely no help.

Mom and Joe were still dancing, this time much more closely, to softer music. They murmured in each other's ears and laughed quietly. I felt like an intruder. Where the heck had aunt Donna had gotten off to? I thought I could count on her at least to stick around to spend time with me, her favorite/only niece. But no.

Nobody was around to make my loneliness less sharp, except…

My eyes slid over to the lounge chair where he sat. Now not only were his sleeves rolled up, but he'd opened the top two buttons of his dress shirt. Goodness. I never thought that a couple buttons on a shirt could make my heart speed up. He looked… accessible. He looked like he wouldn't mind if I sat down and started chatting. We'd never done a thing like that before. He was the grown up, off doing grown up things, and I was… just a kid. But I wasn't a kid any longer.

I must have had just enough gin and tonics to erase my better judgment, because I found myself walking over to sit on the lounger right next to him. I could touch him if I reached out. I hadn't had THAT many gin and tonics, though.

"Hey, Mr. Beaumont."

He turned to face me and blinked. I wasn't sure why. Like he was surprised to see me or stunned or something. He shook his head and his silver hair gleamed in the romantic light. "Don't call me that. Call me Beau."

"I can't call you Beau. My dad called you that." And then I burst into sobs. From out of nowhere. It was so embarrassing. I just couldn't stop.

"Oh," he said, sitting up to face me. "Don't cry, April. I'm sorry. I didn't mean…"

And then he was sitting next to me, with his arms around me, and they felt as good as I had imagined they'd feel. Strong and warm and safe and other things I couldn't identify yet. "I'm so sorry," I sniffled. "I didn't mean to. It's just no one has even mentioned my dad and I felt like-- and when you said that, it just--"

"It's okay," he said, his large hand rubbing my back. "It's nothing. Would you prefer to call me Charles?"

"Charles?" I looked up at him. "Why would I call you Charles?" The very idea shocked the tears right out of me.

He chuckled and touched one finger to the underside of my chin. I tilted my face up. "It's my real name. Would you like to know why everyone calls me Beau?"

I nodded, feeling... something. I didn't know what. Like something was on the edge of happening.

"Well, it was in elementary school. I went to this very small private school, and there were five boys in my class named Charles. So we had Charles, Charlie, Chuck, Trip-- because he was Charles the third, and then there was me. So I became Beau, short for Beaumont. And from then on. Everyone has called me Beau. Even my parents."

"But not me," I said. He smelled good. He smelled warm and spicy and a little like pine trees. It was sexy.

"Not if you don't want to."

"I don't want to. I like having something of you no one else has."

The night stopped.

I knew nothing really had, of course not. Maybe it was only inside of me, and inside of him, too. His eyes met mine. This close, even in the shadows of the night, I could see the light in his green eyes. They drew me in like a shimmering pool. I could drown in them, I realized. Would that be bad? Why did I want to be drowned?

"Charles," I said, settling into his arms. I felt his chest expand with a deep breath. "Charles, am I a bad person if watching my mother be happy with another man makes me feel sad?"

He let his held breath out. His hand was still patting my back. No, I shouldn't call it patting. It was more like stroking. The girls were right. Charles was turning into a lovely distraction.

"Your father wasn't a very good husband, I'm afraid."

I stiffened. "He was a great father." I couldn't admit the times he wasn't there, or was distracted, not when we'd always been a team against my mother.

"Perhaps, but he wasn't... kind to your mother."

"Yes, he was. He was always very nice."

"Nice is not the same thing as kind. He loved her, in a way, but he didn't love her the way he should have. That's why when I met Joe, I thought of your mother. I thought they would..." he paused. "...Fit together. And I knew what kind of husband he was. He loved his wife before she died. I thought your mom deserved someone who would love her for real. You father... he didn't. I understood that about him, and I didn't blame him, but he and I didn't deal with our marriages the same way."

I went silent then. There were things we never mentioned when I was growing up. Things that were secrets. Scandals. Shames. "You're talking about my father's mistress." My voice was small. Quiet.

He didn't answer for a while. "You knew about that?"

"I heard them arguing once. I never asked about it."

"I'm sorry." His voice was quiet.

It turned out I didn't want to talk about it. A lifetime of avoiding talking about my father's mistress hadn't made me want to face it now. Maybe I was more like my mother than I knew. "Why are you sorry? Did you do it too?"

"No!" he answered quickly. As if the very idea was offensive. "I wouldn't. I'm not like that."

"Not a cheater, huh?"

"I've only ever been with one woman. My wife."

I stiffened. "What?" Impossible.

He leaned away from me, his arm dropping from my back. I missed the contact. I turned so that I could face him on the lounge chair. Our knees touched.

He moved his knee. "I don't think this conversation is appropriate."

"Wait a minute. You've only ever been with your wife?"

"We were very young when we got married."

My mind whirled. It was possible, but it made no sense. "Okay, okay I can see that, but you've been divorced over a year. I can't believe that the women aren't all over you. I mean look at you."

He laughed. And his lashes fluttered in embarrassment. They were long and dark and pretty. "I wasn't ready to get into the dating scene, to be honest."

I grinned and nudged his shoulder with mine. "That I don't blame you for. It's a nightmare out there."

"It is. You're a beautiful young girl, you should be careful out there."

I liked the compliment, but the young girl part made me grimace. "You know," I said slowly, my heart beating a mile a minute. "I'm not a young girl. I'm a grown woman."

This time he turned to look at me, his head cocked and a question in his eyes. Wow. He really was gorgeous. Those pale green eyes, bright enough to show through the low light, and his silver hair clipped close about his ears, setting off his long dark lashes. Strong bone structure. I wanted to kiss him. I wanted him to kiss me back. I caught my bottom lip between my teeth and then dropped my head. All my boldness, gone.

"I guess you are." The husky tone in his voice made me whip my head up again to catch his expression. His smile was crooked, as if he was mocking himself, but his eyelids were heavy and the way he looked at me made a heat spread from the center of my being.

"You know, a lot of people would call me a dirty old man in a midlife crisis for talking with you like this."

"You're not old," I started when there was a clatter at the dessert table.

We both jumped. It was Mona and Jack, fighting. They had knocked over a platter of pastries. Had they been fighting all night and I hadn't noticed? "Oh no. I should go stop that." I started to get up when Mona planted her fists on her hips and snarled at my brother. I couldn't hear what she said exactly. I knew that meant it was a problem. When Mona got deadly silent she really was going for the jugular.

Jack smirked. "Oh that's really classy, Mona. You can't argue with my point so you resort to profanities."

"Fuck you, Jackass. Fuck you." Mona threw up her hands and whirled, stalking off down the path to the road.

Jack's girlfriend came out of the house then, looking peeved, and gathered up my brother who still had a look on his face like he had just been enjoying himself immensely. Mona hated when people toyed with her.

"Excuse me," I told Charles, then took out my phone and texted Mona.

me: You're supposed to prevent drama, not cause it. Remember?

mona: Don't worry about me. Your brother's a jack-ass. I'm going back to the hotel. See you there.

mona: or maybe I won't see you there. *wink wink*

me: stop.

mona: don't stop. enjoy your distraction. have fun. XXOO

I shook my head and put away the phone, my stomach fluttering with butterflies. My heart racing. She was teasing me, but I didn't think I wanted to stop. I was enjoying my distraction. I slanted a look at him. It felt like more than a distraction. It felt like something special. I shoved down the irrationality of that.

"Where did everybody go?" I asked. Surprised. The only people left were the waitresses cleaning up the place. Even the bartender was gone. So was Elisa-beth. It wasn't hard to guess where they had gone. What had she mentioned? The outdoor shower. Gross.

"Well, the bride and groom left a while ago. I assume to do what brides and grooms do."

"Don't." I begged. I did not need to think about what my mom and Joe were doing.

He grinned. "Your cousins took my son under their wings and I think they took him into town."

"Oh no. You didn't let Dave and Paul get their claws into Matthew did you? He's such a sweet kid, and they are holy terrors. They're going to corrupt him."

This time he laughed out loud.

"It's okay. I trust my Matthew. He has good judgment. And he's old enough to make his own decisions."

"You're a good dad."

This time he ducked his head at the compliment.

I watched the waitresses clean up after the mess Mona and Jack made. One was tall and graceful with silky straight red hair tied into the perfect chignon that I was always jealous of because my hair always popped out of its ties and looked a mess. Even sweeping she looked composed. The other waitress had her curly brown hair cut short. Probably smart.

She couldn't pull off a chignon next to this one and still look professional. I had sympathy for her. Then, she looked up at me, the short, curly haired one, with huge blue eyes and heart shaped freckled face, and I felt a shock of recognition. Did I know her from somewhere?

She smiled awkwardly and then went back to cleaning up. The momentary shock faded and it was just the backyard, empty. The party was over and I was surprised by the pang in my heart. I didn't want this to end.

"I guess we should say good night, then."

CHAPTER FOUR: CHARLES

I did not want to say good night to her. I did not want whatever was happening between us to end. I didn't care if she was young. She made me feel alive, more alive than I had in years. Everything about her entranced me. Her wit, her openness. The way she'd let out little tendrils of who she really was. The way she bit her lip and blushed like she wasn't as sophisticated as she acted. That long neck and those perfect collar bones..

I wanted to take her hair down and let it free, let my fingers tangle in her brown curls and kiss her like mad until her lips were swollen and she was panting, and then I wanted to make her laugh, to make her feel good, happy...

I hadn't felt like this in so long.

I hadn't felt like this ever.

The image of her, naked in my bed flashed through my mind and before I could think better of it I let the words I wanted to say, the foolish words I shouldn't say, come from my lips. "Would you like to come home with me?"

Her huge dark eyes widened further, rose colored lips falling open, soft and luscious. That blush on her cheeks that brought color to her face. Then she smiled with a quirk and slid her hand into mine. "Yes, please," she said, and let out a soft little laugh.

I laughed, too, and stood, drawing her up with me.

We were only inches apart, her head tilted back, and her mouth offered up to me if I wanted to take it, and I did, but not here. Not yet.

I pulled on her hand, a little tug, and crossed the yard with her trailing behind me. There was no one but the caterers left at this wedding party so no one was there to observe us. This was private. Just us. We went through the dunes to the beach, the short-cut between her family's beach house and mine. She knew the way, of course-- she'd been there plenty during the summers she'd spent here when she was young. But this time was different.

The moon had risen and the sand was cool. The sound of the surf gave everything a dreamy quality. I had to stop, I had to just be in the moment. To pay attention to it, and her. It seemed important to do so.

"What is it?" she asked, stumbling in the sand in her high heels.

"I just wanted to stop for a minute." She blinked up at me and smiled. She looked like a renaissance angel in the moonlight, the breeze teasing those locks of hair that had come loose and been driving me wild all night. "I wanted to look at you."

She lowered her eyes shyly, suddenly bashful. It was sweet. I couldn't resist. I brushed her hair back from her face and cupped her soft cheek. When her eyes met mine my breath caught in my throat. I'd never seen something so perfect. April. She was perfect. I had to kiss her.

She came to me like she belonged in my arms. Her lips were so soft-- warm and generous, yielding against mine. Her body molded against me and a small sound of pleasure escaped from her throat. She clung to me, and I kissed her deeper, my tongue finding the sweet cave of her mouth, and drinking whatever it was that was the source of her. Whatever it was that was filling me up.

One of her hands crept around my neck and her fingers played the hair at the nape of my neck and it felt so good, I hungered for her so much that I gasped.

I pulled back and she clung to me, with a wordless protest, trying to kiss me again.

"April, April," I said, not believing I was about to say this. "Wait, we need to think about this."

"No we don't," she gave up on trying to reach my lips, and ran her lips down my neck, finding my racing pulse and touching it with her tongue. My knees almost gave out.

"This is a terrible idea."

"This is a great idea." She bit my pulse, and I had to resist pulling her tight against me and never letting go.

I put my hands on her shoulders, oh her shoulders, and held her at arm's length. "No, really. Your mother is going to be furious."

April scrunched her nose in displeasure and there

must have been something wrong with me because I found it incredibly adorable and sexy. "She would hate the scandal." She blew that lock of hair, my favorite lock of hair, out of her face. "Okay. We won't tell her. She's not the boss of me. This can be our little secret."

She moved to reach for me again. "Everyone will think I'm an old creep having a midlife crisis and you're just some little chippie."

"They will?"

"Oh, they will."

She bit her lip in consideration. "Okay, I can live with that." She tried to kiss me again and I had to laugh.

"April, I'm serious."

"So am I. We're both single. We're young and free."

"I'm not young."

"Young enough."

"I'm too old for myself." Donna had been right. There was something wrong with me that I couldn't accept this beautiful woman wanting me, that instead I was worried about what people would say.

"Then you need me. I'll be young for you."

"I don't think it works like that."

"It can for us. We don't have to worry about what it means, Charles. You don't have to be that guy everyone else thinks you are. You're Charles. Not Beau. This can be whatever we want it to be and it doesn't have to have anything to do with anyone else. Not my mom or your ex wife, or all those people who will make judgments. It's ours. And we can make it whatever we want as long as we want it. If you want to have fun because you've been serious too long, you can. If I want to..." her eyes ran down my body and then up again, her face flushing in the moonlight, as her lashes fluttered heavily before meeting my gaze, "...go home with the hottest man I've ever seen, I can."

"Your mom was right about you. You're a troublemaker."

"I can be your troublemaker if you want." Her smile was sly and I liked it. This time when she came in to kiss me I let her.

It was the best kiss of my life. Maybe there was something to this younger woman thing. When I stepped back I swore I saw stars. Yes, there were stars in the sky, a whole universe of them, but these were April's stars. They were just for her. "You really want this, don't you."

"I do. I really do."

"Why?"

"Do we need to know why? I'm not sure I know. I just know I do."

I pushed down my misgivings. All the reasons why I shouldn't do this, why SHE shouldn't do this, and I grabbed her hand again. "All right then. I'm taking you home. I'm taking you to my bed. And we'll spend the night making each other happy, and not worry about anything else." A thrill went through me. I was going to take her home and make love to her, and damn the consequences. We could deal with whatever happened.

"Wait!" She pulled back on my hand and let go, holding her hands up to ward me off. "What about Matthew? I don't want to run into him in the morning."

"Morning? My son? Ha. He won't be up until past noon, I guarantee it. Besides, he's taken over the garage apartment whenever he comes out to the beach. He only comes into the main house for food. He wants a bit more independence with his friends."

"Wow. You've thought of everything. There are absolutely no impediments left, besides how far away your house is."

"My house isn't far away it's right over--oh." I grinned at her. This was something we were both willing to do. The risks bubbled through my brain, but I pushed them aside, holding my hand out once again. "Look in my eyes, hold my hand, and trust me."

She inhaled audibly, her eyelashes fluttering over her big brown eyes, then she nodded, and slipped her hand back into mine. I felt a jolt of connection at the feel of her skin on mine. We walked through the dunes to my house as if in a dream. I don't recall opening the door or leading her upstairs. We were just there, in my bedroom and she was in my arms, feeling like she belonged there. We kissed until the room disappeared from the universe. It was just us. Just me and her. The need rushed through me. This wasn't just sex. It wasn't just about how long it had been. There was a kindness about April that I'd never known and that I wanted, desperately.

She trailed her fingers down my face, the depth of her eyes warming me to my soul, then cupped my cheek. "I didn't realize I wanted this so much."

I turned my head and kissed her palm. "Me either. I've never… want isn't the right word, darling. This isn't lust, you know that right?"

Her lips curved into a welcoming smile and I couldn't take my eyes off of them. "What is it then?"

"It's beautiful."

Her smile widened. "Beautiful?"

"Yes, very beautiful." I ran my fingers through her hair and pulled out the pins holding it up-- finally. I combed it out and let the curls twine around my fingers. "Beautiful," I said, bringing it to my nose to smell her scent. Roses and jasmine and a hint of something smoky. Yes. I nibbled at her earlobe, and she shuddered, melting into me. "Beautiful. Everything about you is beautiful. Everything about this night. About us. I've never known such poetry. Your every breath is like a song."

"Oh," the word was a gasp. Her legs buckled and I caught her against me. This time our kiss was deeper, hotter, the warmth catching fire and combusting this energy between us. I was on flame. She lifted one leg to wrap around my hips and struggled with shaking hands to unbutton my shirt. "Please," she whimpered. "Please, Charles. I need you."

The sound of my name on her lips, in her trembling, low voice, struck a chime through me, a resonance that set up a responding vibration. I needed her too. I pulled off my shirt and dropped it to the floor. Her skin was like velvet as I undid her dress, sliding the lacey ruffles down her arms and letting it puddle at my feet. The heartbreaking sweetness of her peachy lingerie made me feel privileged to hold her, to kiss her. I pressed my lips to her neck, ran them down the delicacy of the tendons to the curve of her shoulder. I nibbled at those enticing collarbones, happy to finally taste what I had believed out of my reach.

"Charles," she moaned as I released the fastenings of her bra and let it fall to meet the dress on the floor. I ran my hands down her back, the perfection of her slender, strong muscles. Nothing had ever felt so pure, so right. I had to have her. I had to know her. I lifted her in my arms and she clung to me kissing me so desperately nothing within me could have made me pull away from her sweet mouth.

I laid her gently on the bed and bent over her, kissing her, kissing her like she was my air. Her hands scrabbled, unseeing, at the fastenings of my pants, I leaned back to help her and froze.

"What?" she said, reaching for me, urging me to keep going.

All I could do was stare at her in wonderment. "You are altogether beautiful, my darling. Everything about you. I could never hope for more..."

When she blushed this time, it spread from her cheeks all the way down her chest, making her glow, rosy and enchanting. Oh yes, I liked making her blush. She squirmed with pleasure. "You'd better be careful, Charles. If you keep saying stuff like that, I'm not going to want to leave when the night is over."

I cocked my eyebrow. "Is that on the table?"

"This was supposed to be just one night. A secret... a scandal."

"Was it?" I shed my pants and boxers, and her reaction to that was more a whole body flush than a blush. Even her pretty little toes turned pink. I kissed them and she moaned. "We might have to renegotiate that." But then I began my slow trail up her body, and her ability to negotiate, or even speak more than monosyllabic words, was compromised.

Compromised thoroughly.

⁓

WHEN SHE WOKE THE NEXT MORNING, I WATCHED HER stretch that soft, slender body, the peaks of her round breasts puckering the sheets. She raised a hand to her lips and yawned before her eyelids fluttered open and she found me staring.

I smiled. "Good morning, April."

She beamed at me, happiness suffusing her face. My heart stopped at her loveliness. I was bewitched by her. Enchanted. Completely under her spell and she did nothing but smile at me.

"I've never had such a good sleep," she said. I brushed her hair back from her face. It was now tangled into masses of wild curls that I adored.

"Good."

"I think you wore me out, old man." She rolled over and pressed her body against mine, nuzzling into my neck with her warm, luscious lips. "You surprised me."

"I thought you said I wasn't old."

"You aren't. You are.. you..." She leaned up on an elbow and caressed me. Neck, chest, arms. "That was… uh." She blushed. I couldn't stop from grinning at her blush, I grabbed her hips and pulled her close. "That was something else. I've never.. that was.. amazing. Charles, that was the best sex I've ever had. I thought you'd only been with one woman. You're unbelievable in bed."

I laughed out loud. Her face scrunched at me and that made me laugh more.

She slapped me half heartedly on the chest. "Don't laugh at me!"

I wrapped her in my arms and rolled her so she was on top of me, pressed against me. She wriggled until she could get her arms under her to hold herself up. She wanted to talk. I liked it. I'd never met anyone who said whatever she felt, who did whatever she wanted. Who was just herself, no matter what the world wanted her to be. "I'm flattered but why did that surprise you?"

"You said you'd only ever been with one woman… It made me feel worldly and wise, like I was the one who would be the teacher."

I raised my eyebrows at her. "So the old dog taught you a few tricks, hmm?"

"Stop. Don't make fun of me." Her hair fell over me and curtained both of us in it's shadows.

"I'm sorry," I whispered. I tucked one side of her hair behind her ear. "I'm sorry." I gave her a kiss that was meant to be short but she pursued until it was hot and wet. "Darling," I murmured as I broke it off before it could go farther. "I don't know if you want to get into this more… not if you don't want to be found with me."

"What?" She pulled back.

"It's almost noon."

"I slept until noon?"

"I didn't want to wake you. You were so lovely."

"Matthew's going to wake up soon and raid your kitchen and I'll never get out of here without being seen." She jumped up from the bed leaving me there, cold and suddenly bereft. I did not like how my arms felt empty without her in them. Watching her search for her clothing, a sense of wrongness filled me. Five seconds ago, everything was perfect-- better than perfect. April was in bed with me and the sun was shining and I felt alive, something that I realized I hadn't felt in ages. Now she was rummaging about my room, naked and gorgeous, which was a plus, but still.

"Where the heck is my underwear?"

I didn't want her to go.

I jumped out of bed and picked up her silky little lace thing from the top of the mirror where I'd flung it before feasting on her last night. I handed it to her.

Her eyes met mine and there was that blush. Dammit. I didn't want a one night stand. I didn't know what I wanted, but I wanted more. "You know, I'm leaving the Hamptons tonight. I have to be back in the city on Monday morning."

She didn't say anything, just pulled on her underwear and fastened her bra. I put on a pair of pants while she sought out and found her dress, pulling it over her head and zipping up the back before she even looked at me. She was chewing on her lip. "I'm getting on the train with Mona at four today. She's going to stay with me in Manhattan as her favor for being my date to this wedding. Mom will be here in the Hamptons for her honeymoon, so I'm the host of her fancy New York City vacation." She chuckled and looked up at me guiltily. "She really didn't want to come. Neither did I."

I let out a breath I hadn't known I was holding. "I'm really glad you did come and I wish…"

She took a step towards me. "Wish what?"

"I wish this wasn't over."

She cocked her head at me. "I thought it was a one night stand."

I shrugged. "I don't think that was a requirement."

"I thought we didn't want anyone to know?"

"We don't have to tell anyone at all. We can meet in New York. It's a big city. No one has to know."

"My mom won't even be home for weeks."

"See? It's a good plan."

"You're just happy to be having sex after a long dry spell."

I stepped up and pulled her close to me, chest to

chest. When I looked down, she looked up, willing, happy. I bent and whispered in her ear. "I am happy. I'll keep you happy too." She shivered against me and I loved that I could do that. Everything between us was new and real and joyous. "Is that what you want?"

She nodded, her hands grasping at my back, her desperate clawing making me want to throw her back down on the bed and say to hell with everyone. "But what about your mid life crisis?"

"I deserve one, I think. Divorced dad. Married too young. Long dry spell."

"Not anymore."

"Previous long dry spell, now broken."

She laughed and reached up on her tip toes to kiss me, but before I could get into it she pulled back. "But what about me? They'll call me a floozy."

"Chippie. They'll call you a chippie."

"Oh. A chippie. Okay then. That's all right." She grinned at me. "Give me your phone."

"You want my phone because…?"

"You really are rusty, aren't you? Because I want to

give you my number so you can call me and we can meet in the city."

"Ahh," I said, like she hadn't just caught me being an old man who had no idea how to date in the current world. I gave her my cell phone and she entered her number.

"There, now when you get back, you can call me and we can make plans."

She gave it back to me and I looked at what she had entered. "Chippy?"

She shrugged, cheeky. "That's me, right? Now you send me a text."

"What do I say?"

"Anything you want. That's how I get your number."

"Oh you want my number too? I thought I was supposed to call you so I could take you on a date."

"Oh, Charles. I'm a modern woman. I don't wait around for a guy to call me. Text me."

I could barely restrain my smile, but I did as she commanded.

me: I like you.

chippie: good boy. :)

I laughed. Then she showed me what she'd entered my name as. "Old man?" I was slightly offended. "I thought you said I was young."

"Yes, but that's who we are in this secret affair. We are the old stereotype. Cheap and meaningless. It's awesome. I'm the young chippie and you're the pervy old man. "

"Hey, now."

"Who is REALLY good in bed."

"Now who's pervy?"

"Me!" she growled, and threw herself at me, knocking us both to the bed again. I rolled her over so I could kiss her the way I wanted to. With everything I had. It got hot and breathless very quickly. We forgot that she was trying to leave quietly before anyone discovered her.

A dull bass beat filtered through the room. She sat up, her arm against my chest holding her up. "What is that?"

"Oh," I said. I helped her up and then stood with her. "Matthew's up. He'll be over here soon for something to eat."

"Does he always play his music so loud first thing in the morning?"

"Yes. It's one of the reasons I banished him to the garage apartment."

"You're a wise man."

"Too wise." I sighed. "You have to leave even though I don't want to let you go."

She smiled sadly. "Just for now. I'll see you next week. I'll take you out for falafel."

"No, I'll take you out for a nice dinner."

"It's a deal," she said. Then she gathered up her purse and snuck out the back door, on the other side of the house from the garage.

Somehow I knew that my life had changed for good.

∽

I DIDN'T WAIT FOR NEXT WEEK. WELL. TECHNICALLY it was next week, but in reality, it was the next day. I texted her at lunch on Monday.

me: I can't stop thinking about you.

chippie: I miss you, too.

me: When can I see you again?

chippie: I thought you were going to buy me dinner.

me: I'll give you more than that. Meet me tonight.

chippie: yes

For some reason, that one word, "yes," made me more excited to see her than anything else. I gave her the address of a chic restaurant/bar attached to an even more chic hotel. The rest of the day stretched on interminably until I could make my excuses and leave for the day. Sometimes it was good to be the CEO. I went to the bar and sat where I could get an easy view of the front door so when she walked in, I thought I would be ready.

I was not.

She had dressed for me. She wore a slinky black dress that was held up by tiny straps, her hair tumbling loose over one eye in sexy curls. A blood red slash of lipstick on her mouth spread into a welcoming smile and her sultry eyes fastened on no one but me. If she'd looked sweet and wholesome at the wedding, tonight she looked like a sex goddess. Mine.

She walked over to me and I found myself in front of her without remembering actually standing up or making a move towards her.

I kissed her cheek and she leaned into me as if it were more. I wanted it to be more. I led her to the bar. "Would you like a drink? Our table should be ready in 15 minutes or so."

She sat as I held out her chair for her. "Oh, you mean we're actually *having* dinner."

"Yes. Of course we are. What did you think I was asking you out for?"

Her mouth puckered adorably and her eyes rolled, looking about the bar, with all it's highly polished wood and lacquer. "Well, this is a hotel. Didn't you get a room for us?"

I nearly swallowed my tongue. I leaned into her. "Are you playing the floozy tonight, April?"

"No." She fluttered her eyelashes at me. "The chippie. Don't I look like a chippie?"

"You look beautiful. You look so sexy I could eat you up."

"Good! Then it worked."

"You don't need to dress up and play games to get me to want you, darling." And then it hit me. She wasn't just dressing up for me. She was dressing up for her. She was nervous, and the outfit was camouflage. "Would you like something to drink?"

"Whatever you think is best," she said. The smile hid the nerves.

I was going to do my best to make her relax and have fun. This was supposed to be fun, this thing between us, not scary. I ordered her a chartreuse martini with mint and when it came, she sipped it slowly. "It's good," she said, her voice small and constrained.

This wasn't going to work for me. "Step outside with me, please."

She blinked her surprise but slid off the stool as I led her out to the sidewalk, one hand on the bare back of her dress. We stopped and watched the traffic speed past for a moment, with the lights of the tall buildings far away, and pedestrians strolling. The city was shiny and loud, a direct contrast to the still beach of two nights ago. But she was the same. And I was the same.

April chewed on her lip, pretending not to be nervous, trying to do this thing between us like we'd named it. A secret affair. Dressing up for me. Calling herself the chippie.

I put my arms around her and she immediately curled into my chest. "April, sweetheart, you don't have to pretend to be anything you aren't. I like you for who you are. Please don't be nervous around me."

"I like you, too. I'm so sorry. I must have gotten into my own head and started over thinking things. I do that sometimes. I end up getting anxious over minor things. I started thinking that if we were going to do this thing you'd want something."

"I do want something. You."

"But you're so dignified and powerful. What could you possibly want from me? I'm just a recent college graduate who has no idea what she wants to do with her life. How can you be interested in me?"

"I don't know, April. I don't know why or how this happened I just know it is. And I am interested in you. I find you smart and sharp and funny and fresh and unspeakably lovely. You have your whole life ahead of you and sometimes it feels like mine is over. My marriage ended. My son grew up. Even my business runs so smoothly I scarcely need to be there. But you? You're hope. You're the future. You have dreams and goals and adventures." I breathed in. "You're my adventure."

Her eyes crinkled at me like a smile, but it didn't look like she was happy. "Okay."

"You don't have to be this glamour girl… unless you want to. You're beautiful, but you're beautiful no matter what you dress like. You're the most stunning woman I've ever seen. Inside and out."

"Stop."

"No. I won't. You have dazzled me. Entranced me. Are you a diva?"

She slapped me lightly on the chest. "Only if you make me mad."

I grabbed her hand and held tight with my own. "There you are. There's April. Oh good. I was really looking forward to spending the night with her."

"You are a dangerous man Mr Charles Beaumont."

I didn't want to be a danger to her. "No. I won't ever hurt you. I'm here to take care of you and keep you safe."

Her eyes sparkled and she shook her head at me like she didn't believe me.

"Believe me."

Then she kissed me. Just lightly. And when she pulled back she grinned. "Oops. I've marked you." And then she reached up and rubbed the lipstick of my face.

She had. I was marked all the way down to my soul. She'd called me dangerous but I was the one in danger of losing my heart to her. Completely.

They called us to be seated at our table and we carried our drinks to our delightful dinner of raw oysters and risotto and lamb, but nothing was as delightful as she was. Afterwards I led her up to the room I had booked because of course she was right. I'd taken a room, because I wanted her so badly. I needed to lie with her again, not just to have sex, it wasn't that. I needed to touch her, to look into her eyes, to make her smile, to run my hands through her hair and feel her press herself up to me, as much skin touching skin as possible. I needed her. I needed her so badly I felt off balance, I felt like I was falling.

And when we were in bed, naked and panting now,

exhausted and fulfilled, it occurred to me that this was more than what we had said it would be. It was more than a secret affair. She was no chippie although I might be an old man. If she wanted to keep it a secret, I was going to have a problem, because I wanted to declare this to the world, these feelings, this thing with this woman. I knew I'd have to convince her to let everyone know, and I needed to be patient, until she understood just how important this was, how special, how profound. I couldn't push her.

She fell asleep in my arms and I admitted the real danger, here. It was already too late. I had fallen in love with her.

Far from the old man and his mid life crisis, I was like a young man, maybe the young man I'd never been able to be, thrust into adulthood and parenting too young, and she…

Was my first love.

CHAPTER FIVE: APRIL

*T*wo weeks and one day after my first night with Charles, I woke up in a panic. It was a certainty: My life was over.

I woke up in one of the twin beds in my childhood bedroom, in my mother's home on the Upper East Side of Manhattan, because I had just graduated from college and still had no idea what I wanted to do with my life. I was in no way planning to go to law school like my perfect brother before me, no matter what my mom wanted. But my secret desire to be a painter was not something she would support, and I was no fool. I needed some sort of support for that one. So I was taking a few months off from the impossible decision to have a… something with an incredibly hot man, who just happened to be my dead father's best friend and who was an absolute impossibility in real life. He was just something I wanted. Something for fun. I never seriously had any thoughts this might be real. We joked about it all the time. Pervy old man. Young chippie. My mom would hate it. He was old enough to be my father, if he'd been a teen dad, anyway. It was obviously nothing. Just something for fun. A secret. A lark. Sowing oats. And soon I'd have to stop avoiding reality and make a choice about my life, and then grow up, and it would all be over, just a memory. We would both move on to our real lives. The concept made me panic.

But the question of how my life would take shape out with these conflicting paths and desires was suddenly thrown completely out the window. Because now, all the choices had been taken from me.

I threw my pillow across the room at the other twin bed.

"Hey!" Mona startled awake, sitting up and blinking at me, her hair huge and wildly curled all over her head. "This is my last day in New York City, I deserve to sleep late before I have to go home and go back to work. Do you know what time I have to wake up every day to teach the morning yoga class?"

She threw the pillow back. Harder than I had. It hit me in the stomach and I clung to it.

"Mona, I'm fucked."

She rolled her eyes and combed her hair back with her fingers, lessening the wildness by a degree of just a little. "I know." Then she leaned over, put her glasses on and checked her phone. "By my count, you've been fucked at least a dozen times. Beau must be even better in bed than he looks to keep you this distracted. I think this is the first night you've actually slept here since I came to visit."

I had neglected her terribly. It was true. I got out of my bed and crawled into hers so she had to scoot back and make room for me.

"What the--?"

"No, really, Mona. I'm fucked. I'm really fucked. I'm late."

I couldn't see her face because I had already pulled her blankets over my head, but I felt her still. "Oh shit," she said, and then laid back down with me, pulling me into her arms. "Are you sure? Maybe it's just the stress. Your mom got married. That was a big deal."

"I'm NEVER late, Mona. Never."

"Maybe you're syncing to my period. We spend a lot of time together. I'm not due for another week. How late are you?"

I shook my head against her shoulder. "Everyone else always syncs to mine. I never sync to anyone else's. I get my period every twenty eight days, no exceptions, like clockwork. This is day 29. No period. I'm pregnant."

"Uh uh. Nope. Don't start panicking. You always do this. You always imagine things into the worst possible scenario. You don't know. You're one day late." She threw the covers off of us and climbed over me, shoving her legs into the jeans she'd left on the end of the bed last night. "I'm going downstairs to the drug store and getting you a pregnancy test and you'll see. You're not pregnant. And you can stop freaking out."

I grabbed my boobs. "They're bigger, Mona. And they hurt."

She stopped zipping her jeans and looked up at me, her eyebrows drawn together in a concerned frown. "Didn't you use condoms?"

I sighed and then pulled the covers back up to my neck. "Not the first time. We didn't mean to have sex. I wasn't planning on meeting anyone in a wedding full of family. And he has never slept with anyone but his ex wife. He never hooks up. We used protection every other time." I let out a bitter snort of laughter. "I guess it was too late."

"Wait what?" She sat down on the edge of the bed. "You're the second woman he's ever slept with."

I nodded my head. "Yeah."

"He's practically a virgin."

I widened my eyes and pressed my lips together. No virgin could ever be as skilled in bed as he was. "Absolutely not. He has way more experience than I do. Just all with one woman. Apparently sex was all they had in common. They barely spoke, otherwise. She was his college girlfriend, and just sex was fine then, but not for a life together."

"You're saying he got his college girlfriend knocked up, then lived unhappily with the consequences of that for almost twenty years, then the first time he has sex after that was over he knocks you up, too?"

I could barely breathe. "Oh no. His life is ruined, too.

Oh no. How could I be so stupid. We said this was just a fun thing, just because it made us happy, and it's the first time he got a chance to do something he truly wanted just because he wanted. He raised his family. Now was his chance to live his life how he wanted."

"Please, calm down, April. You stay here. Drink some juice or something, because you're going to have to pee when I come back. We don't even know you're really pregnant."

"I'm pregnant." My voice was monotone. I knew.

Mona just made a face at me and left me to hide under the covers. When she came back with the test, not just one, but three separate tests, I took one.

Mona and I sat there on the edge of the bathtub, waiting for it to turn.

"See, it's not going to turn," Mona said, before time was up.

I didn't say a thing as a faint pink line began to show. We stared at it.

"That's not a line," she said. I just looked at her. Maybe I was the one who turned everything into the worst case scenarios, but she was the one who stubbornly refused to admit when she was wrong. "Take another one. That's why I bought three." She picked up another box, reading the package. "This one says it's the most sensitive for early results."

"Well why didn't we do that one first?"

"I don't know. I've never done this before. Do you still have enough pee in you to do it again?"

I nodded. I'd saved my pee because whatever response the first test had been I knew I wouldn't have believed it. She handed me the box and then gestured towards the toilet.

"Are you going to stay in here while I pee on the stick?"

"Yes. Yes, I am. I have to make sure you do it right."

I looked at her like she was crazy. She probably was. But so was I and I didn't want to argue, so I hunkered down and took the second test.

This one turned positive, a blue cross line, before the time was up. "Look at that," I said. "It is more sensitive. We should give this product a good review." I felt brittle, like I would break at the slightest touch. A whisper. A kind look. A word. "Do you want me to take the third test, too? I'm out of pee. You'll have to wait."

"This isn't the end of the world, April. We can take care of this. We'll get you an appointment at the clinic and you won't have to worry about it. You'll just make sure you are more careful in the future."

Ah. A solution. I should have remembered how practical and down to earth Mona was. She didn't judge. She just found a solution.

So why did that solution that would solve all my problems break my heart?

"I can't."

She was already on her phone, searching for the nearest women's clinic. I put my hand over hers, made her lower the phone.

"No. I can't."

Mona looked up like I was crazy. "Why? You're pro choice. Your body, your choice. You don't have to be terrified of what your life is going to become. You don't' have to regret your mistake."

She was right about all of it. So that wasn't the problem. Then what was it? Why was the very thought of getting rid of it so anathema to me? "Oh no, Mona." I dropped my head into my hands. "Oh. I'm in love with him. I can't because I love him. Because it's his baby. And oh no. Oh. Mona I want it. I want his baby. Oh, Mona. What's wrong with me?"

She sat down on the tub next to me and put her arm around my shoulders. "It's okay. Don't worry. It's not like you have no resources. And he's rich. Super rich. Why don't you call him and tell him you're pregnant. He's a great guy, right? I'm sure he'll do what's right."

I looked up at her in horror, tears bursting from my eyes. "NO! I don't want him to feel bound to me because I have his baby. That's what happened with his marriage and then he was stuck with a woman he didn't love for twenty years. Can you imagine how it must feel, to be trapped in a life you didn't ask for, to do it just because it was the right thing to do. I can't do it."

She stared at me. "How are you planning to keep it from him? He's a family friend. He's practically family. Even if you don't talk to him, he's going to find out through your mom."

"Oh no. My mom. This is the biggest scandal she's ever had to face. Her daughter is pregnant with the child of her dead husband's best friend. We hooked up at her wedding! She will be so pissed at me for that." The tears dissolved into laughter. Was this hysteria? Was I hysterical? "I guess I have an excuse to get out of going to law school after all." I couldn't stop laughing. I slipped off of the tub to collapse on the cool tile floor, and laughed and laughed and laughed.

When I finished laughing, it was just me, breathing, with Mona sitting cross legged next to me rubbing my back.

"So what do you want to do?" she asked me.

"I can't tell Charles. It will ruin his life. I can't tell my mother. It would shame her and break her heart. What can I do to get out of this nightmare?"

She brushed my hair off of my forehead. "This rich people world you live in has too many rules. Everyone has to follow all these social rules. If it were my mom she'd be like," she raised her voice into a falsetto that sounded nothing like her mom, "'every child is a blessing, the more the merrier,' and then she'd, like, feed you homemade kombucha and teach you how to macrame a cradle for the little tot."

"I love your mom. She's always made me feel

welcome." I'd spent many college breaks up in the Adirondacks with her family in their sprawling house. They added a new extension onto the house every time they needed more room, because her dad was a master carpenter and her mom had a tendency to adopt anyone who needed a place to stay and settle for a while. Artists, musicians, hippies, homeless teens. It made for an unconventional home, but a warm one.

"That's because you always are welcome. My parents love you-- oh!"

She stopped. I missed her hand rubbing my back. It was making me feel better. "What?"

"I know what you should do."

"What? Tell me already."

"You should run away with me! Come home with me. You can hide out. My mother is a freaking doula."

"What's a doula?"

"It's a lady who professionally helps other ladies through birth. It's one of those hippie things."

"I can run away from home and live with your

family and my family never has to know and be ashamed of me?"

"You don't need to be ashamed. If they make you ashamed, they're the ones who are wrong. Come home with me, and be with a family who actually accepts you for once. You're awesome. You don't have to fit some debutante mold."

I sat up from the floor and put my head on her shoulder. "I don't think this is the mature course of action, Mona."

"Screw mature. You need to take care of yourself. And I need to take care of you because you're my best friend for life and I'll help you through this."

Tears started again, but these were a different kind of tears. These were tears of love and happiness.

"April honey," she said, patting my hair. I felt like a kitten, and her, the mama cat. "We're going to have a baby."

"You'll be with me?"

"As long as you want me to be."

"Okay," I said. Decision made. I didn't want to think about it too much. I tried not to think at all. I packed some bags and that night we got on the midnight bus to head out to Saratoga Springs, where her parents would pick us up and drive us into the mountains.

Mona was drowsing, her head on my shoulder when my phone chimed.

old man: April, I thought you were coming over tonight. Is everything okay?

I couldn't breathe. No, everything was not okay, I wanted to tell him. I'm pregnant with your child. But I couldn't answer him. If I did, I'd have to tell him the truth, and there was no way that could end well. Either he'd try to marry me out of duty, or he'd try to convince me to get rid of it, which I couldn't do. Or if I was wrong about who he was, he'd dump me and I'd raise the baby alone. I didn't know which option would break my heart more. So I did nothing.

old man: April are you okay?

I couldn't answer.

old man: April?

There was a lump in my throat and I felt hot. The phone rang in my hand. He was calling me.

Mona startled awake. "What is it? What's wrong?"

I showed her my phone and who was calling.

"You don't want to talk to him?"

"I can't." My voice was barely audible. Barely recognizable.

She nodded and took my phone from me. When she gave it back, her lips were pressed into a firm line. "There. I blocked him. You don't have to talk to him if you don't want to."

"I want to, Mona. I love him."

"So talk to him."

"I can't."

And she let me cry into her shoulder for at least the next hundred miles as the bus traveled away from my life.

CHAPTER SIX: CHARLES

SEVEN YEARS LATER

Mickey pulled on his leash as I was locking the door of the brownstone. It was a small brownstone, nothing terribly lavish, but as I was the only resident, it was plenty big enough for me, my 'bachelor pad,' or so my son joked when he came to stay. I might have bought it so that he could come stay with me, out of the limelight, although I wouldn't ever admit that to him. It would make him feel too self conscious. But I loved it anyway, even after he left to go back out to the Hamptons, reluctant to be in the middle of a city, with all the busyness and noise. The tall windows let in the light on the grayest of days, but the dark walls were soothing and sophisticated. Nothing loud or flashy. It had high ceilings and many stairs and narrow halls that hinted at the age of the historic building, and I liked feeling a part of the flow of the past and present and future. It wasn't anything like I'd had growing up or in my marriage, but it felt right. And it had the best views in New York City. Surely a luxury.

I walked with Mickey down the front steps-- now that we were heading in a direction he liked, he'd stopped pulling on the leash-- and enjoyed the Manhattan skyline and the East River splendor along the Promenade. Every time I saw it, it made me feel like I was finally living my own life.

It was not a bad bachelor house, not at all. I was very glad I'd moved out of my immense penthouse apartment in midtown that my ex wife had wanted but never felt right to me, and into my own house with my own walled garden, in a place that felt like a neighborhood. I walked down the tree shaded street-- busy with life on this fine almost-summer morning, with my dog, who was, as everyone agreed, the finest, most handsome shaggy mixed breed goldendoodle with the friendliest face possible, even if he didn't always have the best manners-- and reminded myself that I had a good life.

It was a good life.

I turned the corner, and held on to the leash as Mickey strained to go down the street towards the dog park. "I have to get a cup of coffee first, Mickey," I told him as I stopped at the window. And he settled.

"Your dog is so cute," the girl at the to-go window said. Dressed in her apron and brunette ponytail, she was cute, too. I gave her my best smile. She blinked rapidly, and a bright blush came to her cheeks. "Can-can I get you anything, sir?" she said, breathlessly.

For just a second she reminded me of April and my heart gave a familiar pang before I shut it down. "A black coffee, please, darling. And one of those dog bones for Mickey." I nodded at the jar on the counter. This was a dog friendly neighborhood, and I'd never had a dog before I'd gotten Mickey from the rescue. I liked having a dog.

"Okay," she said, leaving the impression that she would give me just about anything if I asked it. She stood there for a good few moments before Mickey gave a tug.

I turned, ready to lecture the dog on leash manners. He usually didn't listen, but I kept trying.

"Hey mister, can I pet your dog?"

That's when I found out why he was pulling the leash.

It was a little girl. Mickey loved kids, probably because he was mostly a puppy himself. She was maybe fivish years old, with light brown pigtails and huge round purple sunglasses with polka dotted rims. She wore a yellow kermit the frog tshirt, with a bright rainbow, and black and white striped leggings and pink sneakers. It was quite a look. She made me smile.

I pulled gently on Mickey's leash and told him to sit. "Sure, but be careful he can be a little too friendly and I don't want him to jump on you or lick you."

"I don't mind," she said and got down on her knees where Mickey was sitting, tail wagging so hard it nearly made his rear end take off like a helicopter. "Hi, puppy. Hi!" she said.

"His name is Mickey." I squatted down near him, to make sure he didn't get too enthusiastic and knock the small child to the ground so he could love her better. He probably needed to go to obedience school.

"Mickey! Like the mouse! My name is Minnie. Mickey and Minnie. We were meant to be friends,

Mickey." He must have agreed. She laughed as he licked her chin. She looked up again. "I miss my dog, but he had to stay in the country with Grandma and Grandpa when me and Mama and Momo moved to Brooklyn to make our Bohemian Emperor."

"Your what?" I'd forgotten how much fun little kids could be. It had been a while since I'd been around them.

The door to the coffee shop jingled then. "Minerva Hamilton," a sharp, feminine voice scolded. "What did I tell you about running off without me or Momo?"

Before I looked up, I knew. The warm day went still around me. I blinked once, twice, slowly, before coming to my feet. And there she was.

"April," I said, like it was just any other day. "Nice to see you. It's been a long time."

She gaped at me, frozen, which gave me plenty of time to take in the woman who had left me to run off with her girlfriend, now wife, according to her mother, and broken my heart.

I was over it. It was seven, no, seven and a half years ago. Her fresh faced youth was gone. The brown hair whose curls I'd loved to tangle my fingers in was now tied in a frazzled braid that hung down one shoulder of her faded black t shirt. She wore ripped baggy jeans and smudged high top sneakers and juggled two, no, three bags.

But her eyes were still as huge, still as warm and rich, and her mouth had fallen open in surprise, as if she was waiting for a kiss.

I shook my head angrily. No time for stupid fantasies. I could admit she was still beautiful, even if she no longer looked like a young girl. A terrible, sly part of me said I liked her even better as a woman not a girl. She'd filled out, not so lithe and slender. Full breasted and round hipped, she had something to hold on to. When she'd left me without a word, I used to pacify my ego, saying she was too slight, too delicate, like I could break her if I wasn't careful, and a real woman had curves. But even then I'd known it was just sour grapes. I knew it was a story I told myself to hide how it hurt when she abandoned me. It still hurt. But now I didn't have that story to fall back on. She was luscious.

She raised a hand to rake it through her hair, a nervous habit I remembered from years ago, but it got caught in her braid and just left a hank sticking up, endearingly. Her breasts pulled against her t shirt, which was entirely too thin for my peace of mind. I could tell that underneath it, her bra was black, too.

Dammit.

"Here you go, sir," the girl at the window said. "Your coffee." I turned to her in relief. An escape from the long dead feelings of longing for April that I'd thought I'd conquered. The coffee girl was now wearing red lipstick and she smiled invitingly at me.

"Thank you, darling," I said, my voice deliberately low. The blush came back to her cheeks.

"For your dog. On the house." She handed me the dog biscuit.

"Aren't you a sweetheart." I winked at her, and she leaned forward on the window ledge as if she couldn't help herself. I shouldn't have winked. I was aware of how women responded to me. But my awareness of April, not three feet away made me want to show her that I wasn't the celibate fool I'd been when we got together. There'd been women since her. Plenty of women.

"Minnie, would you like to give Mickey a treat?" I asked, holding it out to the little girl.

"Can I, mama?" she begged.

April had regained her composure and she scowled. At me. At Mickey. At the sky. But when she looked at Minnie, her face softened. "Honey, you can't keep running off to play with strange dogs."

"But, mama, he's not a strange dog. He's my friend. His name is Mickey, like the mouse." She rolled her eyes, but gave permission.

I handed her the dog treat. "Your mom's right, Minnie. It's not safe to run off without someone. You should always make sure one of your moms is with you. But you're lucky. I knew your mom when she was little, so I happen to be safe, but you didn't know that when you started talking to me. You shouldn't talk to strangers."

I smiled at April, to let her know just how unbothered I was by running into her and her daughter that she raised with her wife. It was of supreme importance that she think I was unbothered.

And it was of rather high importance that, while Minnie was busy with Mickey and the dog treat, she was back to staring at me again, a stricken expression on her face. She was the one who had left me for someone else. She was the one who should be bothered.

The door jingled again.

A tall slender woman with a loose bun on her head that made her even taller came out, juggling three to go cups. She wore a tight tank top that exposed a great deal of creamy pale brown skin, and a long full skirt that swirled around her ankles. There were little bells tied around her ankle, and the chimed when she walked up to us.

"Your green smoothie, babe." She handed April a cup. "Carrot/Beet for Minnie and Orange/Strawberry for me."

"Orange is mine, Momo!" Minnie jumped up from the dog to collect her child sized cup of orange smoothie.

Mona laughed and teased Minnie, ultimately giving her the orange one and keeping the one that was a lurid red.

I felt my smile freeze on my face. It was hard to present a charming front when your insides were peeling back and splitting you open with jealousy. Mona was incandescent with a beauty only hinted at with the awkward 21 year old at the wedding years ago. She had been pretty then, but now she'd grown into herself. She had a loving family. A loving wife. And I hated myself for wanting what was someone else's. Wanting what was hers.

"And who is this?" Mona asked and I didn't know what to say, I still couldn't speak. I didn't have to.

"This is Mickey," Minnie answered for me. "He's my new friend."

Mona got down and ruffled Mickey's ears. Mickey ate it up. "Oh what a good boy."

She looked up at me and smiled, then stood to greet the human man, instead of the canine. "And this is?"

"Hello Mona," I said.

She cocked her head and looked at me as if she was trying to place me. She didn't recognize me. Why would she? I was just some guy her wife once had a secret affair with.

April slid her arm through Mona's and pulled her to her side. Mona looked at April as if that was odd then her eyebrows lifted in surprise. She looked back at me and took a breath. "Beau."

So she knew about us. That was good. April was honest with her wife. I'd thought she was an honest straightforward kind of woman until she'd left me without a word. It was good at least that she was truthful when it mattered, and it was just with me that she was deceptive.

I nodded.

She looked back and forth between me and April and then her eyes fell to Minnie.

She stood up straight and her pleasant smile was back. "It's been a long time, Beau. What has it been? Seven years?"

"Seven and a half."

"More like seven years and nine months, I think."

"Mona," April snapped. "Let's not bother Charles, I'm sure he's busy."

April was on edge again. I was vindictive. "Not at all. I was just taking Mickey to the dog park. But he's fine." I pointed to my overly friendly dog who was at that moment laying on his back with all four legs in the air as Minnie scratched his belly. They both had wide smiles on their faces, the canine one with an added lolling tongue. "We go to the dog park every day at this time."

"Mama takes me to school every day at this time and we stop by the kid park on the way."

"You and Mickey have another thing in common."

"I wish I could see Mickey instead. Mama can we go to the dog park instead of the kid park every day? I can ride the swings on the way home from school but I don't get to pat Mickey."

"That is such a great idea!" Mona beamed. "April, you should make it a regular thing. Minnie can go to the dog park to play with Mickey every day and get to know h--"

"--Charles. Get to know Charles." April interrupted her.

Mona looked quite self satisfied. "Okay then, it's a date."

"A date?" April and I asked at the same time. How did this happen?

"Yippee! A doggie date! Who's a good doggie? You're

a good doggie! What a good Mickey boy." I stared at Minnie. April stared at Minnie. I stared at April. She seemed awfully pale. The vengeful part of me was happy about it. Was she embarrassed? Good. She wouldn't dare go back on it now, would she? I wanted to prove to her that I was unbothered. That I was mature, clearly more mature than a woman who took off and never even told me why she left. Never even told me that she was leaving. Just, as the kids today said, 'ghosted.' She was the one who ghosted. I was the one who'd done nothing wrong.

"We wouldn't want to disappoint Minnie, would we?" I gave her my best cool smirk. The one that made business men run scared and women come running.

"Or Mickey!" Minnie added. "We're friends now."

"We're friends now, April," I told her, not letting her look away.

"Oh." Her voice was strange. Strangled. "Oh yeah sure. No problem. We'll stop by on the way to school. Okay. It's a date." The last sentence was nothing but a whisper.

Mona was bright and bubbly. Minnie was bouncing like crazy. April grabbed her hand. "Say goodbye,

Minnie, we have to go now. Mona come on, we have to GO."

"Bye bye Mickey," Minnie said as April dragged her away.

Mona looked over her shoulder and grinned cheekily. "Minnie, say goodbye to y--"

"Charles! His name is Charles."

Mona laughed. "Say goodbye to your new friend Charles, too, Minnie."

"Bye bye, Charles, make sure Mickey doesn't forget me, okay?"

"You got it, Minnie Mouse."

They went down the street. I watched them go. Sipping my coffee, with a tight grip on the leash because Mickey most definitely wanted to follow. I understood his feelings.

No. I was not okay.

CHAPTER SEVEN: APRIL

*O*nce we were on our way, Minnie tugged to let go of my hand. She happily skipped ahead of us, singing "I met a dog. His name is Mickey. He is all fuzzy. He's my best friend."

What in the world was I going to do? Charles Beaumont showed up from out of nowhere and now my daughter-- his daughter who he didn't know existed-- wanted to be his dog's best friend.

"So that was an interesting development, don't you think?" Mona tucked her hand into my elbow. "He acted like he thought I was your wife."

"You called me 'babe'." I wanted to make a joke, but the words wouldn't come.

"I call everyone 'babe'."

I shook my head not knowing how to talk about this. I sucked on the straw of my green smoothie as if it were a double tequila and could solve all my problems. It was not. It could not.

She answered for me. "I bet it was your mom. She always hated me for turning you lesbian. I think it was easier for her to blame me for my 'lesbian wiles' than it was to accept that you didn't want the same thing for yourself that she wanted for you. Are you ever going to tell her you're straight and we're not together? That Minnie is like my niece, not my daughter?"

I shrugged and sucked in more green energy.

She leaned into my ear and whispered, "Are you going to tell Beau that Minnie is his daughter?"

I shrugged again. "Is he still watching us?" I could feel his eyes on my back. I knew he was watching us. I was hyper aware of his every motion. I had been since I realized he was there, talking to my daughter. Our daughter. Charles. Was here. Back in my life again. With a dog.

April took a sneak peek back. "Yes, as a matter of fact, he is."

"Oh no."

"You're fine. You can handle it."

"Let's take the long way to school." There was a detour that went down the tree lined residential streets. No kid park. No dog park. But also no Charles standing on the street with my daughter's new best friend, Mickey, watching me. There was a knot in my throat and I felt hot. I couldn't face all those parents at school. I needed a break. A distraction.

"Okay," she snagged the back of Minnie's t shirt. "Detour kid. We're going this way." We all turned the corner and Charles was no longer watching us go. The air got lighter. I could breathe. Just a little bit.

But this street was not quiet the way it usually was. Instead there was a couple standing there, arguing. It was a couple we knew well.

Well, not technically a couple. It was Elisabeth and her arch enemy, Duke. The hot bartender at my mom's wedding. He remained just as tattooed, handsome and rough around the edges as he did before, but he had committed the unforgivable sin, according to Elisabeth, of forgetting who she was.

He had not the slightest clue that he'd slept with Lissie, and she was not going to remind him.

"Veganism is better for your body and better for the planet. My restaurant is going to make this world a better place." Elisabeth's hair was pulled back in a loose ponytail, golden strands falling casually from it. She looked like she'd been working, in her cargo pants and her favorite t shirt with the eggplant and the 'vegans do it better' in block letters. She'd probably just been to the restaurant, working with the chef on the menu. Opening night was soon and she'd been obsessed with getting it together. The restaurant was on the ground floor of the building, Mona's yoga studio was on the first floor, and in the bay window of the first floor, my silver jewelry was sold. It was, according to Lissie, a Bohemian Emporium, and had been the lure to get me and Mona out of the mountains and back to New York City. We all lived on the top two floors, me, my daughter, and my best friends. It had been a dream.

I wasn't one hundred percent sure she hadn't bought the building in this neighborhood simply because Duke was part owner of the neighborhood bar that was across the street. I found myself stopping in my tracks, watching the two of them fight. They seemed to really enjoy arguing. This was a lot better drama to pay attention to than what had just happened outside the smoothie place.

"For who? Rabbits?" Duke shot back at her. "Nobody wants to eat lettuce and carrots all day. They want burgers, and french fries and beer. Like red blooded men and women up to no good."

"You are a barbarian."

His smirk slid into something darker. "You have no idea."

"Hey cats and kittens," Mona said. "Sorry to break up your party, but I need you to keep an eye on April for me while I drop the mouseling off at school, okay?"

Elisabeth and Duke turned to blink at us with the same shocked expression. I didn't think either of them had even noticed we'd come up to them.

"What?" Lissie scrunched her face. "Why?" Then she saw Mona's beet smoothie and her eyes lit up. "Oh yeah. I'll watch her if you give me your carrot/beet smoothie, that sounds wonderfully healthy and delicious."

"Looks bloody…" Duke grumbled.

"It's a deal." Mona handed over the beet smoothie before turning to me. "You stay here with Lissie while I drop off Minnie. I will be back. Don't go anywhere."

I meant to laugh and say okay I wasn't a kid but what came out was more like a whimper. She shook her head and pointed both fingers at me. Then she pointed the same fingers at Duke and Lissie. "Seriously, watch her. Come on kid, let's go."

Minnie was too busy singing about dog friends to notice my imminent break down. Thank goodness. They went off.

Lissie sucked on her blood red smoothie. "Mmmm. Earthy." She grinned at Duke.

"Great, more hippies."

"That shows your ignorance, Duke. I'm not a hippie, I'm a health conscious environmentalist. April is a bohemian, and well, okay fine. Mona is a hippie, but she's like a second generation hippie so she's earned it."

I stared at them.

"Is April okay?" Duke asked.

"She's fine. I told you. She's a bohemian, a free minded artist and single mother. There's nothing wrong with that and if you have a problem with--"

"No." He took Elisabeth by the arms and turned her to face me. "I mean is she okay. She's really pale and I don't think her eyes are focusing."

"What? No…" Then she looked at me and her eyes widened. "Oh my. April." She tucked me under her arm. "What happened? Is Minnie okay? I mean she was just here so… is it your mom?"

And whatever I'd been repressing just broke right through. The ugly sob ripped out of me. It felt like my entire heart had been clawed from my chest. I collapsed in her arms.

She gasped and held me tighter.

"Here, let's get her off the street. We'll go in the back." Duke led them through an alley that I hadn't noticed, and into the cool darkness of his bar. It was quiet and calm, and Elisabeth slid me into a booth where I clung to her desperately and sobbed.

A bottle of water appeared on the table and she opened it, holding it to my lips. "Drink."

I did and the icy cold settled me, reminded me that I

was still in my body, still in the present, not spinning around in space thinking about Charles and what I'd lost. What I'd given up.

The sobs settled. "I saw Minnie's father. He lives here. He has a dog. An adorable goldendoodle that Minnie has decided is her best friend."

I felt the shock go through her. "Beau?"

"Beau Beaumont?" Duke's voice was dark and threatening. "What did he do? I'll take care of him."

I looked up at him. "No, no, don't blame him." I shook my head. "He didn't do anything. I'm the one who did it to him. He doesn't know Minnie is his daughter."

He sat down, suspicious now instead of dangerous. "You kept his daughter from him? That's not good."

"No it's not like that. We just had a fling. It was supposed to be just for fun. He'd just gotten out of a terrible marriage and if he had known, he would have married me out of duty. I couldn't...I couldn't do that to him. I couldn't live like that."

He made a disgusted noise deep in his throat. "Doesn't matter. You need to tell him. He deserves to know his daughter, even if he was just a one night stand. Give him the choice of whether or not he wants to be in her life. Or better yet, sue him. He's a billionaire. You'll be set up for life."

Another sob wracked my chest and Elisabeth folded me into her again. I couldn't think of it, any of it.

"It's not that easy. He is a friend of her family's. Her dead father's best friend. Her mother might never forgive her. It's why she ran off. And she doesn't need the money. She's an heiress or she will be when her grandmother dies. And I'll take care of her if she needs anything."

"Must be nice to be a princess, you can just hand out money to people you care about. Or wait for grandma to die."

I sobbed again. I didn't want my grandma to die.

"What is wrong with you!" she hissed at him. "It's not about the money, anyway. It's about Beau. He's the love of her life, but she was just some young floozy to him. She's been in love with him for the last seven years and has never gotten over him. She's been trying to move on in her life. That's why I got her and Mona to move back to New York with me. I wanted her to get her life back."

"And you always get what you want, do you princess?"

"Yes as a matter of fact I do."

"Want a burger?" he offered. Or snarled. It was more like a snarl.

"No I do not want a burger you asshole. I'm a vegan."

I suddenly had a powerful yearning. "I want a burger." I poked my head up. "Please. Can I have a burger?"

"April!" Elisabeth looked down on me horrified that I would defect to the other side.

"I need a burger. I need to tear my teeth into something. Please. I'm not a vegan. I'm not even a vegetarian, not totally. I just mostly eat a plant based diet because I like it and it's good for me and everyone else is. But I still like meat. Sometimes Mona's dad and I would take trips to the village diner and order the biggest burgers. Well, not sometimes. It was a regular thing. Every wednesday afternoon. It was our thing. I could really use a burger right now, Duke, if you wouldn't mind. Rare. With cheddar and mushrooms and onions?"

He nodded slowly at me and stood, shot a disdainful

look at Lissie. "Her, I like. Burger coming up. Want a beer with it?"

"It's too early--" Elisabeth started.

"Please."

"You got it, April." He started to walk away then turned back, leaning one hand on the table. "I won't say anything, but he's a good guy. You need to tell him he's got a daughter. He's a good father, I've met his son."

I lowered my eyes to the table. The wood grain was dark and scarred. This bar had been here for ages. "I know, I just have to figure out how to tell him. And when. And what I want. And how I feel."

"Hmmph. That's a lot to figure out. You're going to need some proper energy and nutrition to deal with it. I'd better get that burger."

He went off into the kitchen while I sniffled into April's 'vegans do it better' t shirt. "He's not so bad. I don't know why you're always fighting with him."

"I can't help it," she said, as she patted my hair.

CHAPTER EIGHT: CHARLES

I leaned on the fence of the dog park waiting for Minnie, sipping my coffee. I had a good view down the brownstone lined street that she usually came down, but maybe April had decided to take a different route. Maybe they'd stopped at the store. Maybe Minnie had lost her shoe. I remember Matthew was always losing his shoes when he was around five. Maybe Minnie was like that. Maybe that's why they were running late. It was just time getting away from them. Or maybe not.

There weren't that many people at the dog park today. Four dogs total. It had rained all night and though it was not raining now, the park was muddy and the bench was wet. Not a great day for hanging out in a park made of dirt. If Minnie had been mine, I would have tried to keep her out of it, tried to get her to stop at the library or get a hot chocolate instead of visiting the friendly dog and some old man.

Some old man.

They were not very late, only a few minutes, but when I only got to see them fifteen minutes a day, each one of those minutes was precious. I imagined that April, the good mom, had convinced Minnie not to come. I hadn't realized how much I enjoyed her company until there came a day when I was worried she wouldn't come. I raked my hand through my hair and settled my shoulders into my jacket better.

April wouldn't know, of course she wouldn't know, I made sure not to let on, how important their visits were to me, how I kept wanting to ask them to come with me to the street fair, or for ice cream, or for lunch. How I wanted to see them on the weekends, too. But Mona was never invited in my head when I imagined asking for more time. I made sure April could not tell how much I liked seeing her every day. If I made it about Minnie, she'd never know. And if I made it about Minnie, bringing her little gifts, stickers or fruits or little paper airplanes that I'd learned how to fold when my Matthew was tiny, then she would keep coming around. I was wooing Minnie, with my dog and my treats and little magic tricks that stunned the child and made the mother roll her eyes. But that was okay.

Because for fifteen minutes every weekday morning, Minnie would race around the dog park with Mickey while April sat with me and chatted. She was still funny. Still optimistic. Still had that tendency to say whatever she felt, to be real. And I wanted to wrap my arm around her and have her lean into my chest as we watched my dog and her daughter play, and just be. Just be together. Of course that couldn't happen. She was married, and I wasn't like that. And I liked Mona. She was witty and down to earth, not that I spent much time with her. I should spend more time with her. I should invite all three of them to do something. To be friends.

The thought crossed my mind more than once, to invite April and Mona out somewhere, as neighbors or friends, but I couldn't do it yet. I was working on it. I was working on tamping down my feelings and being an adult.

Oh, at first it was awkward. How could it not be? I'd had a brief, bright love affair that neither of us had ever mentioned again, and she was now happily married to the lovely woman she had left me for, with a beautiful daughter that I wished was mine.

One didn't just get over that kind of longing and not have a casual daily meeting be awkward… and yet, although I found the longing to be permanent, the awkwardness slowly faded. But the pain of thinking that I would never, could never have them lingered on.

Mickey ran up to me and dropped a stick at my feet.

"Okay, boy, you miss your playmate, don't you?" I threw the stick and he ran, tongue happily lolling after it. I didn't even repress my sigh. I missed her too, both of them.

"Your dog is really cute."

The voice startled me out of my reverie. A woman leaned up on the fence next to me, a couple yards away. She was tall and thin and blinked at me with wide brown eyes. The wind whipped her black hair and stuck it to her lip gloss. She reached up to pull it back and smiled at me.

"Thanks. He thinks so, too." I gave her that smile that my son kept telling me was a weapon.

If it was a weapon, she must have liked it. Because she drew closer. "What breed is he?"

"Goldendoodle. Or so they said. He was a rescue. He probably got too energetic for the family he had before me." Mickey raced back with the stick in his mouth.

"Ahh. Mine is the corgi over there." She pointed across the dog park, where a brown and white dog was laying, his nose pointed towards all the wonderful smells. "No problem with excess energy for her. She's not interested in chasing anything. I bring her out here to get some exercise but it doesn't work."

Mickey dropped his stick and bounced around it. I picked it up and tossed it again. "This could go on forever."

We both laughed at the foibles of their dogs, and then she moved another step closer. "I've seen you here before with your daughter and... ex wife? girlfriend?"

She was bold then, wasn't she? Asking about Minnie and April, trying to find out if I was single. Why did the question make my heart pang? I tried to think about how to answer that question honestly in a way that wouldn't complicate the situation. I shook my head. That was the honest truth. "They're my neighbors. Minnie misses her grandparents dog, so we meet at the dog park to play."

"Ahh," she said, and sidled closer. "A man who likes dogs and children." This time when she brushed her hair back it was with a little flip. She had pretty hair. Long and dark like a waterfall.

I turned to her, leaned in. I could get to know her. Take her out. See where that went. This would be simpler, wouldn't it?

Mickey began barking like mad and ran for the gate. Minnie was here. She had been bundled with a handmade scarf and a pink and green raindrop raincoat, along with the ubiquitous huge purple sunglasses even though there was no sun today. "Mickey!" she yelled and struggled with the gate. I started towards her.

"We should talk sometime," the girl said from her

spot, still on the fence. I nodded but had no attention left for her. They were here.

I reached the gate and opened it for her.

"Hi, Charles," she said and gave me a quick, casual hug around my waist. "We almost didn't come today." Before I could react she let go. I wished she'd come back.

"Hey, Minnie. Where's your mom?" I said to her retreating back. I didn't like seeing her alone. I didn't think April would let her come alone either.

But it was too late, her attention was already on the dog. She ran for Mickey, who jumped and licked and wagged. They were equally glad to see each other.

April was standing down the street, about three houses back, she looked like normal, her hair in a ponytail and a light jacket and jeans, nothing remarkable to notice. But I noticed. Something was wrong. She was frozen, just staring at me. Even at this distance she radiated tension. Her face was filled with hurt and betrayal. My heart twisted for her.

"April? What's wrong?" I took a step towards the gate, then remembered Minnie there with my dog, who was incredibly friendly but not always in control of himself. I couldn't leave her here without being within arm's distance.

She pasted a smile on her face and started towards me. "I didn't want to interrupt."

"Interrupt what? I was waiting for you." I held the gate for her and fastened it behind her. "You were-- you guys were late today."

She lowered her eyes and then flashed them back up at me. Bright. Sunny. Laughing. Not real. "I wonder if the girl you were talking to would say I wasn't interrupting."

Ahh. She saw the girl who'd come up to me. She'd read the situation the same way I had.Yes, she had been flirting with me. And it had taken my mind off of waiting for her. I didn't want to admit that I had been considering flirting with the corgi girl just so that I could stop thinking about April. I didn't like that motivation within myself. It smacked of using a woman when my heart was stuck on someone else. But then, why did she care? She was happy. It wasn't her place to call me out on flirting with another woman, she was the one who'd left me. But it was interesting. This was the first even slantwise hint that we'd been together, that we were not just neighbors. Yes, she'd moved on, but it was clear to me now that I had not.

My heart was stuck on April. It seemed obvious now in retrospect. It had taken a bit over two weeks to fall for her again, but then, it had only taken two weeks the first time, too, so that actually made sense. That's just the way I was around her. With all the women I had dated after her, trying to forget her, not one had ever taken a hold of me the way she had. Not one had made me feel like she had. Not one was as unforgettable as April.

I had come to the conclusion that it was just the rebound thing. The first woman I'd cared for after my marriage. It was just... me, wanting to be out on the market again and enjoying myself. And the way I'd felt about April was a fluke. But now it was clear that wasn't it. April was The One.

If I was going to be honest with myself, then I should at least be honest that I had never stopped loving April, and it hadn't taken two weeks to fall for her again. I'd fallen hard, instantly, the moment I heard her voice scolding Minnie for running off. I'd known it was her and I might as well have stopped resisting.

But I was an adult. I could see this thing for what it was now.

I scuffed my shoes in the dirt, leaned up against the fence again and took a sip of coffee. If she could be bold, I could too. I looked her in the eye. "We were actually talking about you. And Minnie. She thought Minnie was my daughter and you were my ex-wife."

The blood drained from her face and she swallowed heavily. Her fingers twisted in the hem of her shirt. So nervous. But it was time.

Today was the day we got it out. Today was the day we mentioned the elephant in the room, the big secret that we kept avoiding and would never mention. She and I had had an affair and I was still in love with her. My heart beat hard. I wouldn't let her look away. "That was like a sucker punch, that a stranger in the park could see what was between us, when we have been pretending it didn't happen."

Her eyes were wide and frightened but I wouldn't hold off. I shook my head, at myself really. "But here's the problem, April. The girl in the park has a point. I'll tell you the truth. I'm not the kind of man who longs for someone else's wife, I don't like that, but I do think about what could have been if you hadn't left me without a word and run away with Mona all those years ago. I think about being the one married to you and having Minnie as my daughter and I'm jealous."

I looked away finally. It hurt. It hurt deep inside my chest. "And because I'm not the kind of man to cheat, or to cause someone else to cheat, I thought maybe it was a good idea to flirt back with Corgi Girl, to try and give my attention to someone else, not you, not this thing that I can't have because it isn't mine. But it didn't work at all. My heart wasn't in it. It was with you."

She'd gone silent. When I glanced back up to check on her, she was white as a ghost, and trembling.

"April?"

"Sorry," she said, her voice strangled and a little shaky. "I should have said that we're running late. I promised to let her stop by and say hi to Mickey… and you… but we have to get going or she'll be late for school." She cupped her hands around her mouth and called "Minnie, come on let's go."

"Aww, mama…" Minnie complained from the other side of the dog park.

"We're going to be late." Every angle of her body screamed tension, the desire to get out of there, to get away from me to not talk about the thing between us that was like a solid presence.

"Really, April?" So it turned out she was going to continue to play games. Even if she had no feelings for me at all anymore, it hurt that she would treat me like that. That she would continue to pretend that nothing had happened. Maybe I hadn't meant to her the same thing she'd meant to me. That possibility hurt most of all.

"Sorry." She didn't look at me again, her head bent down, her eyes directed away. She bustled Minnie out of the dog park and down the street as fast as she could without actually running.

"Damn it," I swore under my breath. It figured. April knew very well how to run away when things got too intense for her.

"Neighbor, huh?" Corgi Girl asked me.

Of course she'd been watching. Who knew how much she'd heard. "It might be more complicated than that."

"Right." She gave me a pitying look and bundled up

her corgi in her arms and left the dog park, carrying the dog all the way down the street until I lost sight of her. It was too fat to walk, apparently. Or maybe too lazy

There was no reason to hang around the dog park now. I put Mickey's leash back on and went home.

I was sitting on the floor, on the fun striped navy and white carpet, in front of the fire. I had a bottle of wine, a plate of cookies that Minnie had made with me before I sent her to bed, and Taylor Swift playing softly, because who understood a broken heart better than Taylor?

I just did not know how to deal with any of this, so I'd decided, it was for the best, if I let Charles go. Let him live his life. I was so sorry I had come back into his life and made everything difficult again. And I was even sorrier that getting to know him again had made me just as in love with him as I'd been when I'd forced myself to leave him the first time.

I felt like such a fool. An idiot. A weakling. I felt like

I was at the mercy of these terrible emotions that welled up out of the pit of my heart and drowned me.

I'd thought I'd gotten them under control finally. I'd thought I was ready to move on finally. And I wasn't. It was starting all over again. That was the whole point in coming to Brooklyn with Mona and Elisabeth to create this Bohemian Emporium. Elisabeth would run the way too trendy vegan restaurant on the street level, and Mona would run the way too serious yoga studio one flight up the wrought iron stairs to the second level, and I would work in my little jewelry studio tucked away off this living room on the third level, and then I'd sell my jewelry in the yoga studio. This was supposed to be our chance to step boldly out into life and be powerful, creative women, never mind what heartbreaks and pain we'd lived through in the past.

I sang along with Taylor and drank my wine and ate my cookies.

It was all a delusion. Our plan to leave behind the broken hearts was a failure. I still loved him. I had never stopped loving him. It had happened too fast and too soon and too much, and seeing him again made it all rush back in. It had never stopped. I was haunted by him, possessed by these feelings that weren't-- that couldn't be real. I barely knew him. It made no sense.

Desperately, I flopped over on my stomach to grab my purse from the mustard yellow couch where I'd dropped it, and stretched until I snagged the strap so I could drag it towards me, because standing up would be too much to ask of me right now. I dug around for a few minutes before pulling out a pen and the little notepad where I sketched jewelry designs if they came upon me while I was out doing errands.

I finished my glass of wine and poured another before getting to work. I thought for a few minutes, then started writing. One after another, I filled each little page then tore it out and piled them neatly at my side, in front of the fire. The music shut off abruptly.

"What the hell are you doing alone?"

Elisabeth closed the front door, dressed in her work clothes with her golden hair piled on her head. She tossed her keys with a clang into the key bowl.

I snorted. "I don't need supervision, Lissie. I'm a grown up." I took a sip but my glass was empty. With a grunt I grabbed for the bottle to refill it. But that was empty, too. I stared at it confused. I didn't remember drinking the whole bottle.

"And listening to Taylor Swift, too? This can't be good."

I pouted "I like Taylor Swift."

"Where's Mona? She was supposed to be taking care of you."

"I don't need a babysitter. I'm a stupid grown up."

"Oh, April." She took the empty bottle from me and the empty glass and put them both on the coffee table before sitting down beside me. "Why do we have a fire going when it's June?"

"It's chilly." I did not like the tears that threatened. So I stuck my chin out at her.

She shook her head like she was my disappointed mother. "Mona was supposed to stay with you because you need company today after that scene with Beau."

"No. She had a date with that cute girl from the

whole foods store and she was going to cancel it to stay with me, and I told her I was an adult who did not. Need. Supervision. And I made her go."

"Why do you keep saying you're an adult who doesn't need supervision?" She grabbed a cookie.

"Because, I am an adult. And I have a plan to deal with this situation."

"Oh thank god. I was hoping. And what is your plan?"

"My plan is to make cookies," I pointed at the cookie she was eating.

"Delicious," she said around a mouthful.

"Put Minnie to bed, light a fire because it makes me feel good, listen to some wine and drink some Taylor Swift."

"I think you've had enough Taylor Swift."

I made a disgusted noise at her and rolled my eyes.

"What's the rest of your plan?"

"Here it is. Right here." I picked up the pile of notes. "I wrote everything I need to let go of down in these notes, and now I'm going to burn them up, one by one and once I've done that, I will no longer be tied down to those memories and I will be free of these awful feelings."

Elisabeth blinked slowly at me. She did not seem to think my brilliant plan was all that brilliant. She looked at the notes. I felt like I should stop her but my limbs didn't really want to work. They were too heavy.

She read the first one. "'The way it felt like I was home when I was in his arms.'" She looked up at me.

I had to swallow hard.

"'How no one else has ever compared to him in bed, ever.'" This time her eyebrows were raised like a question.

I nodded my head and bit my lip. God he'd been so good. I still fantasized about it.

"'The way he made me laugh and how I could make him laugh.'"

She didn't look up at me, she just shook her head like I was sad, which to be truthful I was.

"'How whenever I look into Minnie's eyes that are

just like his eyes, I remember how much I loved him all over again.'"

When she stopped reading she looked at me with such sympathy. Pity. "Oh, April. You're in love with him. None of that is going away because you burn up some pieces of paper."

The threatening tears leaked. "You don't know that."

"I do. And I also know that your 'plan' shouldn't be lighting fires in June. It should be to tell him that Minnie is his daughter."

I dashed the tears away. "When are you going to tell Duke that you were the girl he slept with in that Hamptons wedding?"

She scoffed. "That is hardly the same thing."

"You go out there to fight with him every day. Three times a day if you can help it. You start fights with him because it's such a blow to your ego that he completely forgot you."

Oh she glared. "Duke is an asshole."

"Yeah, well, he was nice to me." He made me a hamburger and let me sit in his empty bar until I stopped crying.

"That's because you're pitiful."

I gasped, though it was probably true, and then narrowed my eyes. "Maybe he recognized you, but you've been such a bitch that he is just pretending he doesn't remember."

Elisabeth opened her mouth to respond and I was sure it would be deadly, but it was better than talking about Charles, so I welcomed it.

The door opened. "We have a situation."

Mona stood there, with her hair loose and curly and wearing makeup, dressed in a beautiful wrap dress the color of rubies and sapphires and gold. Her face did not match her date wear. She was frowning, scowling even. She tossed her keys into the keybowl, too, and at the clatter, Lissie and I clambered to our feet, our fight forgotten.

Or Lissie did, I needed to be helped up a bit.

"What is it now? Is it worse than April being a mess and you leaving her to decide enchantments is the answer to her problems?"

"It's not enchantments. It's focused attention. Visualizing a better life. It's symbolic. Oh you, be quiet. Let Mona speak or I'm turning Taylor Swift back on."

"Whatever this is," Mona made a sharp motion with her hands, "we'll need to put it aside." She closed the door and told us to sit. This time on the sofa not the floor. "And I don't know if it's worse, but it's a situation, and it's related to April's problems. No enchantments."

"It's not enchantments."

"No symbolism either."

I reached to pour some more wine. I had a feeling that I was going to need it. "Empty." I said. Pretending that wasn't the second time I had tried to pour more wine with an empty bottle. Elisabeth made a sour face and set it out of my reach.

"Wine isn't going to solve your problems either. You've got to tell him he has a daughter."

I laughed unhappily. "He'll hate me. I can't bear it if he hates me."

"Well…" Mona sat on the stool next to me and held my hand.

"Oh no. What happened? Something happened."

"So I was out on my date tonight…"

"Was she nice? Did you like her?" If we talked about that we never had to get to talking about Charles.

"Stop interrupting, April. I swear, you are the most avoidant person I've ever met. You think I don't realize you picked a fight with me so you wouldn't have to talk about telling Beau? Don't you dare let her distract you, Mona. She doesn't want to face this but she has to."

"She's got to face something now."

"Did you tell him about Minnie?" I grabbed Mona's pretty wrap dress by the collar and yanked her close to me, nearly pulling her off the stool.

"Oh my. No." She took my hand and disentangled my fingers. "Relax, babe."

"Then what happened?" I felt a growl starting in my chest.

Mona shot startled eyes towards Elisabeth.

She pressed her lips together. "You shouldn't have left her alone. She lied. She's not okay. She's pretending she's okay and she's trying to run away, using wine and witchcraft and Taylor Swift. It's very ugly."

"Oh my god! The both of you! Just tell me what happened."

Mona sighed. "It was a very good date--"

"Good, but what happened related to me?" If we were going to make it all about me then let's pull off the bandaid.

"Well Beau happened, that's what."

I laughed. "Beau happened to your date?"

She laughed back. "Yes he did. I took her to Duke's bar--"

"Traitor!" Elisabeth gasped.

"Oh stuff it. Tequila is vegan. And gluten free to boot. And it's a nice place with all those cozy booths out of the sight line of other people if they're not looking, which was fine with me, because I was dying to kiss her."

"You made out with a girl on the first date? You slut." I teased. She knew I didn't mean it.

But she levelled me with a deadly gaze. "That's not what your baby daddy called me when he saw me kissing her."

"No!" Elisabeth breathed in gleeful shock.

"He saw you kissing another girl?" I blinked at her. This couldn't be good.

"Yes he did. And he called me a cheater and berated me for having such a wonderful wife and treating her so abominably and he couldn't countenance my behavior."

"He said 'countenance'?" Elisabeth was even more shocked at that.

I shrugged. "He's a little old fashioned." I was clinging to Mona's knee and couldn't let go.

"He certainly does not support cheating, especially on you, babe." The corners of her lips turned up just a little.

"He knew my dad had a mistress, and he always felt guilty that he allowed that to happen, even though I don't know what he could have done to stop it. He introduced my mom to her new husband and I have to admit, she is so much happier with someone who loves her right. He must have felt responsible for me because of that."

Mona cocked her head to the side. "Aww, Babe, you actually think this is because of your dad? It's not. I don't think he even thinks of you as your dad's daughter anymore."

Elisabeth picked up a cookie. "I agree with Mona. I've had quite a few family dinners with him in attendance while you were away in the mountains, pretending you didn't have his daughter. He never talked about you as one of the kids in seven years. He talked about the kids all the time, but all the others, not you."

"He didn't talk about me." I didn't know if that hurt or if it was a thrill of relief. If he hadn't talked about me there must have been a reason. Maybe it was just anger, but maybe it was something else.

"Actually no. He didn't. But he paid attention very sharply whenever you came up. Especially in regards to your marriage with Mona here."

"You know we're not married." I was digging my nails into her knee.

"Of course not, and you swore me to secrecy, but your mom thinks you're married in 'one of those lesbian things' that she thinks doesn't really count, and while she might be homophobic, Beau is not. He thinks your marriage with Mona is real."

Mona plucked my hand off of her knee and put it on the arm of the sofa. "He did think our marriage was real anyway. And he took it seriously."

"Why--why are you speaking in past tense?"

"Like I said. Beau happened to my date, said I was married and a cheater and chased her off. I liked her Mona. Duke had to pull him away and put him in the stock room to calm down, but that didn't calm me down. So I followed him in there and straightened him out."

"You DID tell him about Minnie."

"No, that's your responsibility to do and frankly, it's past time. That man cares about you. And he couldn't bear to let your heart get broken by a terrible wife."

"You're not a terrible wife, you're the best best friend."

"Hey!" Elisabeth complained.

"One of the best best friends."

"And THAT is what I told him. That your mom just assumed we were together because I was bisexual. And you let her because you didn't want to deal with your mom's prejudice towards single moms on top of that. I told him I thought honesty was the best policy, but that I was supporting you in how you wanted to deal with your family."

"He knows we're not married?"

"He knows we're not married."

"What did he say?"

"Not much. He sat on a keg and got quiet."

I sat back. "What does that mean? What does he think?"

"I really don't know. He apologized to me for making assumptions about my character. And thanked me for taking care of you when you needed a better family than your own."

"He thanked you."

"Yes. Thanked."

Mona and Elisabeth went quiet then. They both looked at me, waiting for me to say something. I didn't know what to say. I didn't know what to do. I had been clinging to this fake marriage with Mona because it protected me from my real feelings for

Charles. If I was with her, then I couldn't be heartbroken by him. I couldn't WANT him.

But it was all a lie.

I wanted him so much and he was going to hate me when he found out that the reason I'd run away from him was because I was pregnant with his child.

I had been afraid. I had been young, very young. Frightened and reactionary, I'd made an immature decision. If I had it to do over again, I would have told him when I found out I was pregnant. But I couldn't go back in time, and with every passing year, keeping her from him became a worse and worse choice.

Watching him with her now, my regrets billowed out, filling my heart. Minnie could have had a father all this time. And Charles could have had a daughter. Whether or not we ended up together, I'd stolen his daughter from him, and now I realized how much that would matter to him. He would not have wanted to trade his daughter for his freedom and I had made the choice for him.

"I don't know what to do," I said.

"We can't tell you what to do. You have to figure it out for yourself." Mona patted my hand.

"Screw that. Tell Beau Minnie is his. You have to tell him."

Mona nodded her head and made a gesture, conceding the point. "Well, yes. That is also true. you have to tell him."

I huffed a laugh, a one hundred percent non-humorous laugh. "So you won't tell me what to do but you're telling me to tell him he has a daughter."

They both nodded.

"Let's put it this way," Mona said, her dry voice both sympathetic and no-nonsense. "We're not going to tell you how to do it, or when, but you have to tell him. It's the right thing to do."

"I hate you both."

"No you don't. You love us." Mona wasn't even fazed by my hate. I could always tell her anything and she knew what I meant.

My heart dropped. "When he finds out I stole Minnie from him, he's going to hate me."

When they didn't respond to that, didn't offer me

hope or sympathy or say that he wouldn't, all the fear and sorrow and regret rose up in my chest and broke free in a terrible sob. I cried and couldn't stop it. Mona slid onto the couch on one side of me and Elisabeth held me from the other and the two of them held me until I wore myself down.

"If he hates you, it couldn't be worse than how you feel now," Elisabeth said, rubbing my back.

"It could though. He could try to take her from me."

They both gasped. "He wouldn't!"

"Why not? I took her from him. Why not take her from me?"

"He's not like that. You should have heard how he berated me for tearing your family apart by cheating. He said it would hurt Minnie. He wouldn't hurt both of you by taking her away from you."

I shrugged and sniffled.

"Hmmph." Elisabeth. "That's not going to happen."

"He's a billionaire. If he wanted it to happen, it would happen."

"No way. He's a billionaire, but you're not impoverished, as much as you refused to reconcile with your mother and her support. You chose to live in the mountains like a dirty hippie."

"Hey!" Mona interjected. Elisabeth ignored her.

"If he tries to use his money to take Minnie, then you go to Minerva herself."

"Grandmother? I can't. I'm not talking to my mother. I rejected them."

"Do you think Minerva cares? Barbara drives her nuts, although she likes her better with my dad than yours."

"You seem to know my family better than I do."

"I didn't run off. And Minerva likes me. We meet for tea."

"Did you tell her about me?"

"I promised I wouldn't and you know I wouldn't break my promise. She respects your distance, but she always tells me to give you her love. And if you needed her help to protect your daughter, she would crack open that bank vault of hers and stop at nothing. You should talk to her."

I wiped at my eyes. Was I crying again? "Maybe I should."

"So have you decided what you're going to do?" Elisabeth asked.

I sighed heavily. "I'm going to tell him."

Mona hugged me. "Oh good."

"How?" Elisabeth asked.

I shook my head and flopped back onto the couch. "I have no idea."

*T*he rain and chill from yesterday had blown over and it was a beautiful day again. Mickey ran happily around the dog park chasing a black lab. I'd shown up early, because I couldn't help myself, but, somehow, I was not expecting April to show at all, not with the way she'd run off when I'd told her I still had feelings for her.

And not after what had happened between me and Mona last night. I shouldn't have had so many drinks at Duke's bar, but I thought I was safe from April there. And then Mona had come in, with another woman and it was clear they were on a date. I'd seen red. My fury rose. I slammed my drink down on Mona's table until they broke apart and stared at me as I scolded her for betraying April. I'd felt like a lunatic, seeing Mona with someone else, thinking April would be gutted when she found out. I'd made a scene.

I should feel embarrassed that Duke had to drag me off to stop the nuisance, but I wasn't. I was too infuriated at the thought of April being hurt. I wanted to protect her. I felt responsible for her, even if she wasn't mine. I felt like she was.

I'd had to admit to myself that my feelings for April went beyond jealousy or a crush or any of the things I tried to tell myself to lessen it. Two weeks many years ago had been enough to make the connection. The seven years apart had not been enough to break it. And these last couple of weeks? Those had proven to me that this love I felt for her was irrevocable.

And then finding out she wasn't married to Mona.

I snorted into my coffee. I was still wrapping my mind around that. She and Mona weren't married. They weren't lovers or girlfriends and they'd never been anything but platonic best friends. Why had she let me believe they were a couple? Why had she told her mother that they were? Or had she? Barbara complained endlessly about how April never told her anything... but she also complained about her "lesbian lover" endlessly also. Maybe that was why.

Maybe she didn't want her non-lesbian status to get back to her mother, just to piss her off.

But still. I'd thought we'd had enough of a connection that she'd tell me the truth.

Clearly she didn't. Clearly she let me think she was with Mona so that I'd leave her alone. I felt like an idiot. I had a headache from drinking too much last night. The coffee wasn't helping. Corgi Girl wasn't there, either. There wasn't even an uncomplicated flirtation to take my mind off things. Smart woman. She took one look at this mess I was in and ran for the hills.

I leaned back on the bench and stretched my legs out, watching Mickey play and refusing to look down the street to see if they were coming yet. They would or they would not, and looking for them wouldn't make it happen. I'd just about reconciled myself to never seeing them again when I heard Minnie. It was five minutes early.

"Mickey!"

I whipped my head around. She was struggling with the gate again. I was there in two steps to let her in.

"Charles! Thank you." She gave me that quick,

breathless hug around the waist again, but this time I got to hug her back before she ran for my dog.

April was down the street again. Three houses. Close enough to make sure Minnie got into the park and I was there to watch her.

"Oh, Charles," she said, a fake cheerful smile on her face. "Can you watch her for a minute? I forgot her school bag. I'll just run home and get it and be back to take her to school."

"April."

"I didn't want her to miss out on her time with you. And Mickey. I'll be back, okay?" She looked a mess, actually. Her hair was all over the place. She couldn't stand still. Her smile was tight and brittle. If she would just sit and talk with me we could figure this out.

"April."

"Will you watch her. I swear I'll be back in a few minutes."

So this was how far she'd go to avoid talking to me. Fine. "Okay. I'll watch her. Don't worry about her."

For a second, her smile was genuine, then it cracked and I saw the sorrow.

My heart leapt and I almost went to her, but she whirled and raced away.

What could I do? I latched the gate and went back to sit down and watch Minnie and Mickey play.

Today Minnie was wearing rainbow striped leggings and a purple dress with a pink heart design. She only had one pony tail, but the ubiquitous large sunglasses actually matched her dress. I had to smile. I loved her kooky looks, as if she put on whatever made her happy that day and she didn't much care what people thought of it. And when she laughed, it filled me with joy.

She was a good kid. April had done a good job with her, even if she was all alone. It struck me suddenly that April had been a single mom, she hadn't had a partner like I thought she had. Like she should have had. If I'd been around I would have--

No. That was a bad train of thought. Clearly April didn't want to have anything to do with me. It wasn't even just a matter of being taken. It was me specifically who she'd run away from and avoided and lied to. It was me who she didn't like.

Minnie and Mickey finished their race around the park with Mickey winning, to flop down at my feet panting happily two seconds before Minnie climbed up on the seat next to me.

"Can I have some of your juice?" she asked me.

"It's coffee." I raised my eyebrow at her.

"Can I have some of your coffee?"

I laughed. "No. Little kids aren't supposed to drink coffee. It stunts their growth. And you won't get big and tall."

Her mouth made a wide 'O' and then she settled back and thought about it for a moment before leaning forward again. "But my birthday is coming. And I won't be a little kid soon. Then I can have coffee."

"You won't like it."

"You like it.

"That's because I'm an old man."

She nodded again because of course that made sense. "Can you come to my birthday party if you're an old man? It's next week."

"I would be delighted to come to your birthday if your mom is okay with it."

"I think my mom wants you to bring Mickey, though. Then you can come."

"Oh your MOM wants me to bring Mickey, okay. Then I'll bring Mickey."

"Hurray!"

"So how old are you going to be this birthday? Thirty five? Thirty six?"

"Nooooo." She laughed. "I'm going to be seven years old, you silly billy."

"Seven! Oh my, you're so old. I thought you were only five."

"I'm not a little kid." She wrinkled her nose. "I'm small for my age. My mom says I'm a late bloomer, and it's not because I drank coffee. I'm just like her. She said she didn't look her own age until she went to college. Everyone always thought she was a little kid." She sighed philosophically. "I'm gonna have the same problem. People always think I'm five."

"A late bloomer? Yeah, I guess she was a late bloomer. She always looked younger than her age."

My memories went back to summers in the Hamptons, watching her play with my son, bossing him around when I came out on the weekends, a tiny, spunky little thing. We hadn't bought the house until she was a teenager, but she never really looked as old as the other girls her age. Mattthew barely even thought of her as a girl, but that was more about Matthew. She was a tomboy and slight and small. That might have been why I was so shocked when I saw her at the wedding and she looked perfectly grown and... perfect.

That wedding was seven years ago and I still remembered how she looked.

I stopped and looked at Minnie. She wasn't five-ish as I'd thought. She was six-ish about to be seven next week. The wedding was seven years ago.

More like seven years and nine months ago.

That's what Mona had said to me. I remembered it quite clearly. And how April had gotten angry at her for saying it. I thought it was because of what we'd had together but now...

It had been seven years and nine months since I'd seen them. Since I'd been with April.

My heart was beating too hard. My breath was laboring in my lungs.

Minnie didn't notice that my world had just turned upside down. She was back on the ground, rubbing Mickey's belly as he rolled around, loving it.

She shoved her sunglasses back up her nose.

"Hey Minnie Mouse?" My voice was calm and quiet even though my mind was racing almost as fast as my heart.

"Hey Charles." She didn't even look at me.

"Why do you always wear those sunglasses? I've never seen you without them." Then she looked at me.

"It's because when Mickey met me, I was wearing them. And if I take them off, he won't know who I am and I don't want him to forget I'm his best friend."

"Who told you that?" That was patently ridiculous.

"My mom. She makes sure I have my sunglasses every time I come to play with Mickey."

"Oh she does, does she?" I had a sinking feeling that April had had another motivation for having Minnie

wear sunglasses whenever she was around my dog--
and me. "I think your mom forgot about how dogs
use their sense of smell the most. And even if you
take your glasses off, he'll still know you by how
you smell."

She looked up, happy. "Really?"

"Really." I swallowed. "Why don't you try taking
those off and you'll see he won't forget who you are.
He'll still know you."

She took off her sunglasses and handed them to me
without even looking at me. My heart was in my
throat. Somehow I knew. I knew.

"Do you know me, Mickey? Do you boy?" He
jumped up and immediately began licking her face.

"I told you he'd know you. You're his best friend."

She turned a beaming face on me and the entire
world stopped. Her eyes were a brilliant pale green
with a dark rim, framed by thick dark eyelashes and
eyebrows. I knew those eyes because they stared
back at me every time I looked in the mirror. Everything else about her looked like her mother, but
those eyes were mine.

I was Minnie's father.

She went back to playing with Mickey, completely unaware that my life had been turned upside down.

Minnie was my daughter.

I stared, shell shocked. Unseeing. Unmoving. I felt a hot spill on my thigh before I noticed that the coffee cup, still in my lax hand was tipping, staining my jeans with coffee. I swiped at it. I shook my head. I took a sip. Going through the motions of real life while my brain was whirling too fast to really make sense.

Minnie was mine.

When April left she was pregnant. Did April leave because she was pregnant? We'd only been together for two weeks, that seemed too soon to be able to tell anything, it couldn't possibly be why she left.

She couldn't have left me because she found out she was pregnant. She wouldn't have done that to me. She wouldn't have taken it on all by herself. But had she?

And then lied about having my daughter for seven years?

Anger shot through me. She lied.

She looked me in the face and introduced me to my daughter. And didn't tell me she was my daughter.

I wanted to throw something. I wanted to yell. I wanted to shake my fist at the sky but instead I just sat there, sipping my coffee and watching my daughter play with my dog.

She didn't know I was her father. She didn't know.

A knot of emotion caught in my throat and I felt tears come to my eyes.

That would not do. I fumbled for the sunglasses I had hooked onto my collar and put them on. When April came back, I didn't want her to know I knew. Not yet. Not until I could grasp the enormity. Until I could figure out what exactly I felt beyond rage.

Some unknown instinct caused me to look up from Minnie and there was April, walking determinately towards us down the street. She stumbled slightly when she saw me looking at her, but I slid her a smooth smile, the one I used in the boardroom, that did not let any of my strategies through. A poker face, I'd call it if it were anyone else but me, because I was not a gambler. I was a planner. I made sure things went my way.

April suddenly seemed intensely interested in the ground. It must have been fascinating pavement with how she stared at it so intently. She squared her shoulders and kept coming, as if coming to her doom. Oh she didn't even know.

"Minnie, darling," I said, feelings for my daughter unfolding within me in an unnameable way, out of place for this situation, not yet, "how about you put your sunglasses back on. Your mother's coming. Let's surprise her later about how Mickey knows--" I choked, the word caught in my throat, "knows who you are."

Her eyes were striking, clear and honest and pure. She nodded, not suspecting my ulterior motives. Some day she'd learn to dazzle with those eyes, but not today. Today she bobbed her head happily and stuck the giant purple sunglasses back on her face.

"How do I look?" Her grin was broad and joyous.

"Like Minnnie Hamilton." She should be Minnie Beaumont. I turned away trying to control my emotions, turned to April, who had just come to the gate. The anger made it easy to go cold. I was furious at April.

She smiled nervously at me. "Hello, Charles," she

said and then clapped her hands before addressing Minnie. "I have your backpack. Come on, time to go to school."

The coward. The little coward. She was going to ignore everything and pretend I hadn't confessed my feelings for her. Pretend I hadn't found out Mona was her platonic friend, not her wife. Pretend I was not Minnie's father. Pretend, as she had for seven years and nine months, that she had run from me and lied to me rather than telling me the truth. She was going to bustle Minnie off to school and ignore it all.

"I'll walk with you." I stood, all my attention on my deceitful little ex. I had forgotten how small she was, so I used my height to intimidate. I wanted her to be uncomfortable. She should be uncomfortable.

"What?" Her face went slack before she gained control over her lies again.

"We're done in the dog park for the day, so I'll walk with you and..." he almost said 'my daughter,' "Minnie to her school. Like neighbors do." Because that's all we were to each other, wasn't it?

"Oh, you don't have to. There's no need." April

fidgeted, her hands flinging out in unnecessary motions as if chasing off a moth.

"I'm sure you think so."

Her jaw worked as if she wanted to say something, wanted to snap back. She switched Minnie's backpack from one shoulder to the other then smoothed her hands over her hair which was still a mess. Her half hearted brushing didn't help one bit. I smirked. She nodded once. "Minnie will enjoy Mickey's company. She talks of little else besides him."

It was lovely how I was ranked in importance and that burned. I snapped my fingers and held out the leash. "Come, Mickey, let's walk the lovely ladies to school today." He actually came to me without jumping around. I attached the leash to his collar and he stood with his goofy smile watching us all. Perhaps he knew that he'd get to stay with his beloved Minnie just a little bit longer and that was what he wished. I pushed my sunglasses up the bridge of my nose and tossed my now cold coffee in the garbage.

"Shall we?" I asked politely, enjoying her huff of annoyance and how she could not refuse my polite

and neighborly offer to escort her and her daughter-
- our daughter-- to school.

"Fine." Her voice was tight. Her face was tight. Her movements were tight. Everything about her was tight and uncomfortable.

I opened the gate and held it for them to go through, fastening it securely on our way out.

"It's this way," she grumbled and took Minnie's hand.

Minnie took my hand and smiled up at the both of us.

"I want to show Mickey my school." She tugged on my hand and hugged it to her and I was glad she had something to say because I couldn't speak. My daughter.

"And I want to show my friends Mickey, they're going to love him, Mama."

"That's great, sweetheart," she mumbled, clearly not meaning it but doing better than me being able to speak. But then, she had already known I was Minnie's father, hadn't she? It wasn't a shock and revelation to her, was it?

"That way when Mickey comes to my birthday party, he'll know other kids than just me."

April shook her head. "Mickey can't come to your birthday party, honey." She looked up at me with that tight, uncomfortable smile of hers. "Sorry, Charles. Minnie is dog crazy. I didn't mean to impose."

Didn't mean to impose? She was my daughter. It wasn't an imposition. I suddenly had words again. "I accepted the invitation on his behalf. We'll be there." Impose. She should have imposed on me long ago. Seven years and nine months ago. I felt a heat in my head. Fury. Or was it sorrow? "Unless there's some reason why you don't want me to come."

She met my eyes for the first time today. They were sad. She gave her head a tiny, almost imperceptible shake. "No. Of course there's no reason why you shouldn't come. Please. You're welcome to come."

Her sadness sank into me like a fish hook, working its way into my gut. She was sad. Dammit.

I looked away from her because I didn't want to see her sadness. I didn't want to feel it. I didn't want to be upset that she was sad. I didn't want to care.

I let Minnie pull us down the street by our hands. So did April. Bitterness rolled through me. We were a family. Mother, father, daughter and dog. This had been denied me for seven years.

I hid behind my sunglasses and moved one foot in front of the other while Minnie chattered on and on. Before I realized we were at her school, a large brick building with a chain link playground on the side.

Minnie strolled through the crowd at drop off, proudly telling everyone about her best friend Mickey, and how he was coming to her birthday party. She'd collected quite a crowd of six year olds. I could see now how she was the smallest in her class. Would I have noticed her age and the timing of her birth if I'd walked her to school before this instead of playing proud and coy and jealous with April. Maybe.

April stood back and watched Minnie, scarcely looking at me, while the other mothers crowded around Minnie and me and Mickey. I introduced myself. It was easier with them. Smiling and being charming. April was watching the clouds for some reason. Standing back. Separate.

Then the bell rang and Minnie was called in to school.

"Hugs," April called. Minnie ran up to her and hugged her tight, then kissed her cheek.

"Thanks, Mama." she said and before I could think she had turned to me. Hugging me tight and kissing my cheek, too. I wanted to never let her go. "Thanks, Charles, thanks for bringing Mickey."

I got down to her level, on my knees. "Anything," I said. "Anything you want. All you have to do is ask."

This time she threw her arms around my neck. "I love you!" she cried and I could not, I could not speak or move.

Then she three her arms around Mickey's neck. "I love you too!" She murmured into his ear some things that we were probably not supposed to hear, but I got to my feet and watched her laugh and wave and head into school.

I stood next to April with Mickey at heel. Or maybe she stood next to me. I was not sure who moved to be nearer the other, but there we were, standing next to each other, watching our daughter leave.

"You sure are popular with the mothers," April said. It was like a joke, but there was a cutting edge to it.

"You'd be surprised by how much the ladies liked me." I kept my smile fixed. "Or maybe you wouldn't." I shot her a glance. She couldn't see my eyes through my mirrored aviators, for which I was glad, I was still feeling everything too intensely, but she must have known not to press me.

"Sorry." She bowed her head.

She should be contrite. "We need to talk." I didn't know what else to say.

She nodded her head solemnly. "Not here."

"Your place then."

"God no. Mona and Lissie are still there, this early."

"Then mine." I would not be put off.

She paused. Thoughts rolled through her mind, I could see them, but I had no idea what they were. The world had blown open. She could be thinking about anything. She nodded without a word and I collected Mickey, making my apologies to the children who wouldn't go into school because they wanted one more pat.

Mickey loved it. I thought he would definitely be tugging on his leash towards the direction of the elementary school from now on.

I didn't speak, but gestured for her to follow me. We walked in silence all the way to my brownstone on the Promenade. And yet, walking with her, side by side, even without words, felt right. It felt like something was falling into place. Something that belonged there. Something between us that made sense. Maybe we could figure this out. Maybe I could understand how I felt.

"This is a really nice house, Charles." She stood before the steps looking up at the three story building.

"It's not very big."

She laughed. "Are you joking Charles? This is an amazing neighborhood with world class views."

"It's rather old."

"Historic is the word."

"And the rooms are tight."

"Charles, seriously? When did you get to be so snobby."

I cocked my head at her. Was she teasing me? I realized I'd missed that.

"I like it better than my penthouse in Manhattan. I like the smaller rooms, they feel human sized. And the stairs are a pain, but I can close off the ones I don't use until my son visits. He prefers smaller spaces now. But it's better. I just got lost in the penthouse. "

"Oh yes," she said. "I remember it. It was very shiny and impressive."

I looked down at her, suddenly seeing her not as the woman of today but as the girl of seven years ago, happy in my arms.

"It turns out I don't mind not being so impressive, if I get to be happy."

She gasped on the inhale as if she couldn't get in enough air.

"Would you like to see the inside?"

Her nod was shaky. "Yes please."

I showed her up the stairs, my hand hovering above the small of her back, not touching her. I couldn't touch her right now, and let her in the front door.

She laughed as she looked around the foyer and the open rooms she could see from here. The living room, the library, a bit of the kitchen. The stairs went up and the landing had a sitting area. "When you say it's small and the rooms are tight, are you comparing it to mansions?"

"They offered me many mansions when I was searching for a new home. They were all bigger and much more luxurious. I chose this one. For the views, but also because it felt like a real home."

She laughed again, this time her eyes were wet with tears. "You've lived too long with too much money, Charles. You need to be grounded in the real world."

"Are you offering, April?"

We stood in my living room. It felt right to have her there, but she was so tentative, like a deer ready to bolt.

She wrapped her arms around herself. "We should talk, Charles."

Finally. "Yes we should. Would you like a drink."

"It's very early."

"Yes, it is." I nodded, feeling the weight of the revelations of the last twenty four hours. "Would you like a drink? Because I would."

"Thank you," she said.

"Please have a seat."

I turned to the bar and poured her a drink. Tequila, like I remembered from seven years ago. I always kept fine anejo tequila in my bar even though I didn't drink it, because she had liked it. I had never forgotten. There was a lot about her I had never forgotten. A lot about her I remembered on a regular basis because she had always been in my life, if only as a memory. April liked tequila. So I stocked tequila.

I had pictured her here in this living room, with the dark slate blue walls and black book shelves, the deep soft sofas and the art on every wall, because on some level, I had always imagined her here. In this room. Because I had bought it.

For her.

With my back to her, while pouring her drink in the silver rimmed vintage glassware, I closed my eyes, admitting to myself how much of the last seven years had been about April. About losing April. About wishing she was back in my life, in my house, in my bed. She'd lived in my heart the entire time, whether she'd left me or not. I didn't have a choice.

And now she was the mother of my daughter. We were forever connected, no matter what happened here today. I was angry, but more, I felt like I had an empty place inside of me that she once filled. She had left me empty, denied me her place in my life and mine in hers, and now there was Minnie to consider. She'd run away from me, and then chosen to keep me at a distance.

It was time to have this out. I turned to face her.

CHAPTER ELEVEN: APRIL

I was alone with Charles for the first time in seven years and nine months. I had to fight against the urge to throw myself in his arms, collapse into tears, and cling to him as if I'd never let him go.

I didn't. I was proud of myself. Instead I stood in the middle of his living room and stared at his back as he poured drinks. His house seemed like a place he had settled into, a place to be private and real. The walls and bookshelves were painted a deep, soothing blue, but it didn't feel dark or oppressive. The tall windows and high coffered ceiling let in the sun and air, and plants in the window made it feel alive. The deep cushioned leather sofas looked inviting and there were interesting things everywhere I turned, art, books, pottery, antiques.

I liked it. It felt comfortable, but dignified. Nothing flashy, but unique all the same, hinting back to tradition but also going its own way. Like him. It gave me warm feelings that I really should put away. Now was not the time to have feelings. They might wash me away.

"Did you not want to sit?" He asked when he turned back from the bar with two glasses in his hands.

"No. I mean yes." I sat. "I was just taking everything in. It's a lovely home, Charles."

He nodded in acknowledgement but said nothing as he gave me the glass and then sat himself, crossing one leg over the other and stretching his arm out over the back of the seat, totally at ease. He took a sip, waiting expectantly.

I was here to explain the lies about Mona, I reasoned. Just that. I didn't have to tell him everything yet, but here he was waiting for me to tell him about a thing he already knew, and I couldn't. Not yet. It was too close to the deeper truths below. Lie after lie I'd told. I couldn't break open the truth right here right now. I was afraid it would all come tumbling down.

I took a sniff of the drink, wondering what he would

bring me so early in the morning. It wasn't wine. "Tequila!"

"Anejo." His eyes were heavy lidded and watching me, sending small thrills of long dead feelings through my frame. His voice, though, was cold and emotionless. The corner of his mouth quirked up, just slightly. Not humor, not amusement, like he had a secret that he wasn't telling me. Like he was holding something over me.

I ducked my head and took a sip so I didn't have to face those secrets he had, knowing how many I had myself and how big they were. And how scary. "My favorite," I murmured.

"I know." That voice. Still cold, but cold like a pit that opened up in the earth, threatening to engulf me.

I ran my hands over a throw pillow, feeling the velvet knap, smooth when I patted it one way and rough in the other direction. It was a deep blue, but shimmered with a peculiar silver. It almost matched the silver in the chandeliers and sconces, hung with geometric prisms that struck brilliant lights, in the deep calm of the room.

It was like a moonlit night, I realized. It reminded

me of that moonlit night, the one where Charles had first kissed me on a beach-- dark, serene, expansive, beautiful, and resonating with my soul. The night, I understood now, where I had first fallen in love with him. Oh, I hadn't recognized it at the time, but that was the point when attraction slipped over the edge and fell into the infinity of a love for him that would never end.

I'd had seven years and nine months to think about it, to recognize that it had never been just a fling, at least for me, but rather, an opening of my heart to the man who would own it forever. Whether he wanted it or not. Whether I wanted him to own it or not. It just was. Like the sky was blue. The ocean was deep. The facts of April Hamilton. Charles Beaumont owned my heart.

And now I'd lost the fiction of my fake marriage to Mona. I felt like my chest had been torn open to reveal my beating and bloody organ, vulnerable. Was I now supposed to just hand it over him to destroy as he had every right to do, since I had left him, without a word, so many years ago?

I snuck a look at him. He hadn't said a word. He was still leaning back on his leather sofa, the top two buttons of his shirt open, shadowing a line down his chest that I wished I could press my face to so I could smell his scent. I missed his scent. It had faded in my memory, but I remembered how it made me feel-- warm, protected... loved.

His eyes glinted silver-green at me under his lashes as he waited for me to do something. Anything. I was frozen in memories and fear and desire. I took a deep breath to brace myself and then tossed the entire glass of tequila back in one go.

That got him to speak. "That is anejo. You don't gulp anejo, you sip it." He sounded offended. I almost laughed.

Finally, a human reaction. I shook my head, straightened my spine and turned to face him on the opposite couch. "We need to talk."

"I know. That's what I told you outside the school." He levelled his brows and cocked his head, his lips compressed into a no-nonsense line that I didn't remember from our time together, when we both had been soft and lovely and open. He was not soft and lovely and open now.

Because he wasn't mine I realized and I needed to make peace with that. He would be angry when the secrets came out and I had to accept that. I had nothing to lose anyway, well not him, since I didn't have him, but maybe still Minnie.

Fear leaped into my throat. Okay, not that, not yet. One awful secret exposed at a time.

"I'm sorry I let you believe that Mona and I were a couple."

He raised one eyebrow and took a sip without speaking. Dammit he was not making this easy on me.

"I know that you saw Mona with her date, and I know you thought she was betraying me." My throat was tight and my mouth was dry and I tipped the glass up to my lips to get the last drops of tequila. Dammit, I wished I hadn't drank the whole thing in one go.

"Should I make some coffee?" He asked.

I blinked at him. "Why would you do that?"

He huffed a laugh. "Because it's polite. And you seem to be struggling to get the words out. Perhaps something to drink would help but you tossed back that tequila without thinking." That one corner smile was back, perhaps it had never gone. Wry and snide, and not really amused by anything being said, more by some failure in myself. He shook his head and sighed, putting his drink on the coffee table and standing.

I did not know how long I sat there without speaking before he'd gotten frustrated and given up. He went back to the bar, which looked to be built from an antique safe-- it was fascinating, I'd have liked to take a closer look.. He brought back the bottle and poured a measure into the glass still in my hand.

"This time sip it, darling. It's too early in the morning for shots and this is too fine a liquor."

I would have responded, but he'd called me darling. That was what he used to call me, and my open, bloody heart started pulsating with yearning again.

The bottle went onto the coffee table and he sat again, picking up his glass and gesturing towards me. "You were saying? Mona was it? Is that what we're starting with?"

"Right." I nodded. "Mona. You thought she was cheating on me, and you defended me."

"What? No."

"Yes. You thought she was betraying me, and you

came to my rescue. Thank you, you didn't have to do that."

"That's not what that was about I wasn't--" He stood up again and began pacing the room. "Is that really what you think we have to talk about? How you lied about being married to Mona?"

"I didn't lie. I never told anyone we were married. I just let my mother assume and she said it."

"And you never corrected her because...?" His green eyes bored into hers.

"I didn't want her asking questions. I didn't want her judging me."

"She judged you anyway. And I assume Elisabeth knows and kept your secret all these years. Because she didn't say a word."

I ducked my head and took a sip, a small sip of tequila. I was already starting to feel it. It was loosening my muscles and making me forget the reasons why I couldn't tell him anything, all the things. "Yes, she knew."

"She knew." His nostrils flared. His glare deepened. He growled low in his throat and began pacing again. "She knew." He walked away into the kitchen.

I could see him through the small breakfast bar area. He poured a glass of water from the tap and stood at the sink, drinking it. He poured another and then came back into the living room, fury radiating from every pore. He put the glass of water in front of me. "Drink it," he commanded, his voice deadly. I was shocked. I'd never seen him so angry. He was cold and forceful and dangerous. I drank the water. It turned out I was very thirsty. I drank half of it in one swallow. He was still glaring at me.

"Your mother doesn't know, but you do, Mona does, Elisabeth does. Does your brother? Anyone else?"

"My brother and I haven't communicated much lately. We don't really talk so no. He never asked. But everyone in the mountains knows Mona and I aren't together. Never have been. I'm straight, Charles. Only my mother cares, and she's so weirded out by Mona that she thinks she turned me gay or something. Why would I ever clarify for her my own sexual preference when she's being homophobic towards my best friend?"

"Really April? You think that's what is going on here? I can't believe you."

"Why are you so angry that I let my mother believe I

was married to Mona? I know it was wrong but I didn't do it to you. It was just a white lie."

"Why did you leave me?"

"What?" I stopped. Sputtered. "What does that have to do with anything?"

He ground his teeth together. "I thought all this time that you left me to run away with your girlfriend. I was hurt that you wouldn't tell me, or at least say goodbye, but I had to accept it. We'd always said we were just a temporary thing, just for fun. I couldn't get mad at you for that, could I? But that wasn't it, was it, April?"

He stalked around the coffee table to stand in front of me, glaring down at me.

"Wasn't what…?"

He grabbed the pillow that I was hugging to my chest and tossed it away, then placed one hand on either side of my shoulders, on the back of the couch. Leaning over me, he asked again. "Why did you leave me, April?"

His presence was overwhelming. The breadth of his shoulders filling my personal space. The intensity of his flashing green eyes. The way I could see his whiskers coming in. He must not have shaved this morning, and they glinted silvery on his defined jaw. And his scent. I had forgotten his scent. Warm, spicy, and a little bit like pine trees. I swallowed hard. Struggling. "I--I was scared. We were getting too serious. You were too old-- I was too-- I, Charles..." my voice faded out, smaller and smaller, giving him the excuses I had given myself. The excuses I had dreamed up to tell him in case this ever happened. There were a dozen more and none of them were true. The lies wouldn't come.

"April. Please." His anger broke, and his flashing eyes seemed lonely and sad and hurt.

I couldn't help it. My hand floated up without my conscious control. I cupped his face, his dear, sorely missed face in my palm.

His voice was pained. "Why did you leave me seven years and nine months ago, April?"

I drew in a ragged breath. He knew. I pulled away from him and clutched my hands together in my lap, numb. My fingers were clenched so tightly they were turning white. He knew. He knew. "You're going to hate me."

"Tell me."

I bowed my head and cried. I had no pride left. I had no words. Or I had the words, but I couldn't say them. I couldn't take that last step and admit the truth.

He sat on the coffee table in front of me and took my hands in his. That's it. He just held my hands and waited for me to be ready. He knew, and he waited for me to be able to say it. The very thought of how kind and supportive he was made the tears flow faster. This was what I had denied Minnie. Her father, who would have loved her. No matter what might have happened between us he would have been a wonderful father. I didn't believe we would have stayed together, or if he'd married me he would have come to resent me the same as he did his ex wife. He would only have been with me for the baby, our marriage would have been loveless like theirs and I couldn't bear the thought of him feeling that way for me. It would have been loveless like my parents. He would have hated me. He would have turned away from me and treated me like I had trapped him.

"I didn't want to be a burden to you." It was a whisper that made its way out.

He put his forefinger to my chin and lifted my head.

"Tell me." It wasn't anger anymore. He looked tired and sorrowful. It was how I felt too. "Why did you leave me, April."

I couldn't look at him when I said it. I closed my eyes. "I was pregnant. Minnie is yours."

I didn't move. Neither did he. His breath puffed on my cheek. Slow and steady, like he was trying to control it. Then his finger dropped from my chin. I opened my eyes to meet his, staring into mine, as if for answers.

"Why didn't you tell me?"

How could I answer that question. I wasn't sure I understood myself, I was so panicked. "I was afraid."

"Of what?"

"Of everything. I couldn't tell my mother, she'd want me to get rid of her, and I couldn't. I was afraid you might want me too, also."

"I would have done whatever you wanted. I would have taken care of you."

I tilted my head and considered him sadly. "That was part of the problem. You would have done your duty, just like you did with your ex wife, with whom you'd been trapped in a loveless marriage for decades. I couldn't live like that."

"Like your parents."

I wiped more tears, frustrated now. "There's no point in wondering what could have been now. The decision was made. It's in the past. Why I decided to do it is besides the point."

"I suppose it is. You made your decisions not to be with me and to keep me from my daughter."

My heart stuttered in my chest. "I did--I didn't do it to keep you from her. She wasn't even a real person when I left, just an idea, a fear, a potential. And I was a scared kid."

"You were an adult. We had that discussion."

"Well I was overwhelmed and immature, then. Okay? I admit it. Running seemed like the best option."

"And the nine months before you had Minnie where you didn't inform me I was about to be a father?"

I shrugged. "I was just going from day to day. And I wasn't doing well. I was sad all the time and exhausted but I had support. I wasn't alone. I had

Mona and her mom and dad, who accepted me and loved me more than my parents ever had. I had a home. Do you know they already had a nursery set up, because I wasn't the only unwed single mom to come to them for refuge. It was safe."

"You didn't need refuge! I would have been there for you!" He snorted and stood, raking his fingers through his hair. "You didn't have to love me, April. I would have taken care of you and Minnie anyway, and I can't believe that you thought I wouldn't. I thought you knew me better than that."

I had to laugh. "You think that's what this was about? You think I ran away because I didn't love you? No. I ran away because I loved you so much I couldn't bear the thought of trapping you, of you hating me like you hated your wife. Or how my dad hated my mom. Maybe it was wrong, maybe it was stupid and juvenile. But it wasn't because I didn't love you."

He stared at me. "You loved me?"

"Couldn't you tell that I was in love with you, Charles?"

"I thought maybe. But I wasn't sure. We never talked about it."

"Yes, well we weren't supposed to fall in love. It was stupid of me, the chippie, to fall in love with you. We knew it was just for fun, right? Just a secret affair." I felt like a fool, seven years later. "Don't worry. It was a long time ago, right?"

But he was still standing in front of me, staring at me, his brows drawn together in concentration.

I cleared my throat. "We can introduce Minnie to you as her father whenever you're ready. You can spend time with her as her father..." A horrible thought went through me. "unless you don't want to be her father." I felt my face get hot. I'd kept him from her, he hadn't even known she existed, but the thought that he might know and then reject her hurt me, hurt me so much I could barely breathe. Then I realized. That was why I had run. Because I had feared his rejection. Of Minnie, of me.

"Don't be ridiculous. Of course I want her. I want her all the time. I want the seven years I missed her back."

Oh no. This was worse. "You want to take her from me?" My voice was small and high. My biggest fear.

"What? No! What are you talking about? I would never do that to you."

"But I did it to you." I spoke barely above a whisper.

"I won't." He said. "I wouldn't. I'll work with you to find a way to spend time with her. I have lots of free time now that I've stepped back from my company ever since Matthew almost died--"

"Matthew almost died?" What? "When? Is he okay? What happened?"

"He's fine. Is it okay if we talk about it later and deal with the current crisis?"

"You'll still want to talk to me after this is over? You don't hate me?"

He chuckled unhappily, looking down at me with unamused eyes. "I don't know if I hate you, but I'll still have to talk to you. We have a child, and from now on I want to be her father. In whatever capacity I can."

I nodded. It was what I deserved. "I'm sorry. I was afraid. Sometimes I think I have been afraid my whole life, and the only way to protect myself was to run away or avoid or pretend it wasn't happening. That's how we dealt with things in my house and I was trying to avoid being like my mother, but I ended up being just like my father."

I inhaled deeply. I was just like my father. "Did you know that my father had a secret daughter with his mistress?" I finally met his eyes, needing his answer. It had been the scandal of my childhood, the secret we never talked about, my father's other family. A thing we pretended didn't exist.

He looked down this time, shamed. "I did."

"Have you ever met her?"

"When she was a child. He... your father brought his other family to a golf trip we went on. She looked a bit like you did, but with blue eyes. I didn't like being put in the middle like that. We had words. He never brought them again. I'm not sure that was the right decision."

I gasped and covered my mouth, having trouble breathing. I was shocked at the betrayal that raced through me. He owed me nothing. After what I'd done to him? Why should he have told me my father's secrets? But that didn't matter, this hurt as much as it hurt when I found out my father had another family. It hurt more. Why would it hurt more? "No," I whispered. I shook my head as if denying it could rewind time and keep my father from having another family, keep Charles from lying.

"I'm not your father, April. I'm not like him. If you'll let me, I'll be Minnie's father, I'll be whatever you want. She's my family. I won't hide her away. I won't lie to you. We don't have to be like them. I'm not like that."

"But you were. Just because you didn't cheat didn't mean you weren't the same. You didn't love your wife either. You were only together for your son. I didn't want that."

"You should have told me you were pregnant. You wouldn't have been alone. And I wouldn't have stayed with you just because you were pregnant." He rubbed his hand over his jaw. "You weren't the only one who fell in love seven years ago."

"You loved me?"

He cocked his head and repeated my words back to me. "Couldn't you tell that I was in love with you, April?"

I thought back to those days, those very few short days when we were together, and I could still feel it. "Yes, I could tell," I said quietly. "But I didn't trust it." My breath caught in my throat. "I didn't trust you."

His arms dropped to his side and silence fell as we stared at each other. He raised his brows. "I suppose you were afraid I was like him. I suppose we didn't really get the chance to know each other as adults. I suppose...I suppose it's my fault you got pregnant."

"What? No. I was careless."

"We were both careless, but you were so young. I was not. I knew what I was doing. I know how to practice safe sex. I have ever since I got my college girlfriend pregnant and had to get married. I should have been more careful, but I wanted you so much, and I was swept away by you. That was my responsibility. And I failed."

I blinked up at him. I wanted to touch him. I wanted him to hold me. But he was standing six feet away from me, keeping himself distant. "It was mine too."

"But you were the only one who was held accountable for your mistakes. I was not." He took a step towards me and stopped. "You should have... Why didn't you...?"

"I can't change what I did, Charles. The mistakes

piled up on top of each other. The lies. I didn't know how to climb out of it all."

He took a breath as if he was going to say something that would tear me to pieces but then he stopped, shook his head and sat next to me.

Finally.

I could feel my body yearning towards him, wanting to melt into him, but I held myself back.

"But, April, why did you let me believe that Mona was your wife?"

"I told you--"

"No. Not why you let your mother believe it. Why, when we ran into each other two weeks ago, you let me... you led me to believe Mona was your wife." I remembered how I clutched at Mona and clung to her, practically hiding behind her so he wouldn't know the truth.

All my secrets were coming out. It was terrible. I felt like I had no defenses left. He could demolish me if he wanted. His pale green eyes were warm though, and wondering, the anger faded. He was turned on the couch so he could face me.

I looked away. "Charles, I…"

He turned my face back to him and let his hand rest there on my jaw. "You didn't need that lie. There was no reason for it. Unless there was. What was it?"

"I was afraid." With him so close, so sympathetic, touching me, it was like magic. The lies started to unwind. I wanted to tell the truth.

"Of what. Of me?"

"Yes. No." I didn't know how to explain. "I was afraid that you would be able to tell…" I paused, trying to stop hiding and running, trying to work up my nerve. He was still so handsome. He hadn't aged a day since I was first in love with him. I'd once had hope that he wasn't as perfect as I'd remembered him. Or that he'd changed into someone who wouldn't still own my heart and soul, but no. He was the man I had fallen in love with. "That I was still in love with you. That I am still in love with you."

He drew back, blinking. His lips fell open in surprise.

"Don't," I said, rushing to fill the silence. "Don't worry. I won't ask anything of you. It's just me. I am aware that I'm full of fantasies and romantic dreams that have no place in reality. I just can't shake it. I've never forgotten you. I've never moved on." She suddenly couldn't hold anything back. He would never hate her as much as he did for stealing Minnie from him, so she had nothing to lose in getting the whole thing out. If he thought she was pitiful and delusional maybe that would make him feel sorry for her rather than angry. "I haven't been with another man since you. I couldn't. First I was pregnant. Then I had a baby. Then my friends wanted me to move on but no one compared to you. All I could see was you. I couldn't do that to someone else. I couldn't. So I didn't. I haven't even kissed another man."

He opened his mouth getting ready to... laugh at me? Argue? I stopped him.

"And not a woman either. I told you. I'm straight. I just had no heart left for anyone else. It's always been yours."

"It's not."

A tear rolled down my cheek and I had to laugh. "I know. Don't you think I know that? It's not your heart. It's my fantasy, don't worry."

He put his other hand to my cheek so he could hold

me firmly, so I couldn't look away. "No. That's not what I mean. I mean it's not just you."

I found myself clutching his wrists. "What?"

"April, darling, I'm still in love with you, too."

"You're in love with me?" I couldn't believe him. It couldn't be.

He nodded and wiped my tears away with his thumbs. "I never stopped." He smiled and my heart filled.

I still couldn't believe it. I put my fingers to his lips, just to make sure this was real. He kissed them. His breath on my fingers, the warmth, the delicious rasp of his unshaven scruff, the nearness of him, it broke me open. And inside was the sun. I pressed my forehead to his, sliding my hand around to brush the short hair at his nape. "I missed you."

"Ahh, darling," he breathed. "I missed you, too."

When he kissed me, his lips touched mine, softly, like feathers. He was so gentle, but I wanted more, I wanted him. I pressed into him, giving him what he didn't ask for, opening to his tongue, wanting to be consumed if he would have me. "Please," I begged.

"Are you sure?" He brushed the hair back from my face.

"Please." I kissed him again, climbing on top of him to straddle his lap. His fingers clutched at my hips. "I need you, Charles, please."

"Shh," he said. "Shh," and he stood, with me clinging to him as he carried me through his house and up the stairs.

"You don't have to carry me."

"Yes I do, because I'm not letting go of you again." His voice was low and shivered through me.

We reached the top of the stairs and I couldn't keep myself from kissing him as he carried me, blindly down the hall and into his bedroom.

I didn't care where I was, nothing mattered, all I cared about was that I had him, his arms, his lips, his warmth. I kissed his neck, relishing his scent, and the pounding of his pulse. He lay me on the bed and before he could pull back, I was unbuttoning his shirt.

"You're eager, aren't you."

"Seven years and nine months, Charles, you have no idea how eager I am."

"Ahh, darling," he said, then kissed me passionately, pulling the tie from my hair, to run his fingers through it, tugging on it just enough to send a frisson through my body. I peeled the shirt from his shoulders trapping his arms. He sat back and whipped it off as I pulled my tank top over my head and started on my jeans.

He jumped off the bed opening the drawer of the bedside table and withdrawing a condom. He held it up for me to see. "Nothing we do here tonight will be accidental, do you understand me April? This is a choice we're making. Whatever we decide to do later is separate, but this, you and me, this is our choice. And you have to be honest with me."

I blinked. "Yes, Charles. I'll tell the truth. I swear. I never wanted to lie to you." I reached out my hand to him. "I regret it. I have regretted it every day for seven years and nine months… I just didn't know how to fix it."

"We fix it together, okay?"

"Yes." He stripped out of his jeans and then pulled mine off with one motion before coming to lie beside me, his large warm hands sliding along my dips and curves. He nibbled at my ear while his fingers did wonderful things to my body.

"You are so beautiful," he murmured. "So sexy, my beautiful April, my love." His tongue made its way down my neck to my chest and he took my nipple in his mouth, playing with it in a way that made me gasp.

"Do you like that?" he asked, his voice husky and sensual.

"Yes, please. Oh, Charles." I was panting already, squirming for him to touch me more, to take me.

He smiled against my breast as his hand wandered where it wanted to go. His fingers touched my heat, and my head fell back against the pillow, my hands clung to his shoulders, wanting, needing. "Yes…" I gasped as he skillfully led me higher and higher and suddenly I was screaming, and hanging on to him as if I would float away without him. "Oh," I cried. "Oh Charles."

When I came back to myself, he was watching me, a pleased smile on his face. "I've missed that."

"Oh," I said, dazed, "I'm so sorry. That was so quick. I

guess it had been so long, all you needed to do was touch me and I was ready."

"What are you apologizing for? That was glorious, I love that you want me. I loved how you panted, and grabbed onto me and screamed. I intend to see that all a lot more."

I still had not caught my breath, or he took it away again, I wasn't sure. "What do you want me to do for you? I might be rusty but I think I can remember."

He leaned up on his elbow, looming over me. "Oh, I think what I want from you is to see your skin flush with pleasure." He ran one finger down my chest to my nipple then down my stomach and around my navel. "And I want to hear you gasp," he slipped his finger into my center as I obliged him. "I want to taste the sweat from your longing," he nipped my jaw, then kissed down my neck. He raised himself over me and I spread my legs to cradle his slender hips, feeling his erection heavy between them. I reached down to guide him in. I wanted him now. "I want to smell your arousal, and I want to feel," he grunted as he thrust into me. "you around me."

We both moaned at how good it felt. He stilled on top of me, adjusting his weight.

"Kiss me," I begged. And he conceded. He kissed me until I didn't know where I ended and he began, and as he moved in me, the world that I had always known finally settled into something that made sense. I was his and he was mine and this was as it always was meant to be.

I did not know how long I felt the heat rising inside of me. It spread from my center out until I was one incandescent being.

"April, my love," he murmured, his touch and his voice and his smell and his body filling me up until I came again, gasping in his arms, as he followed me over the edge into bliss.

CHAPTER TWELVE: CHARLES

*A*pril's skin glistened and her soft lips opened in ecstasy. I watched her the whole time she came, drinking in the sight of her, like a parched man in the desert at an oasis. Thirsty, coming back to life. I had longed for her for so many years and she was back in my arms. Nothing had ever felt as right as being inside of her, and I groaned as her body convulsed around me. I rode her orgasm into my own until I went blind with it and the world faded away.

I collapsed on top of her, weak and spent. Lost in reaction. I came back slowly, first noticing her hands stroking by back, sliding over my shoulders and down, playing a harmony on my ribs and smoothing the small of my back. They came to rest on my ass.

"Charles, you feel so good, I missed this so much," she was murmuring, I didn't even know if she knew what she was saying. "I love how you smell and the feel of your hair and how strong you are and how you make me want to open up my chest and give you my heart to keep and not worry about breaking it because it's yours, love. It's yours." There was a little hitch in her voice that made me wonder if she was about to cry.

I shifted, realizing I had collapsed on top of her. "Oh, darling. I'm too heavy. I must be crushing you."

"No," she shook her head. "I like how you feel on top of me."

Her fingernails clutched into me. And the slight pain sent a zing of desire through me. A low laugh broke from my throat. "Oh really?" I combed her rich dark hair back from her face, happy to have the loose curls twining around my fingers again, after so many years. "You do? Show me." I rolled over and took her with me, laughing, until she was draped across my chest, her plentiful curves molding to my body. "Mmm. Yes. You're right. This does feel nice." Now I could get my hands onto her ass, soft and firm at the same time, and curved to fit so perfectly in my palm.

I settled her more firmly against me and nuzzled her neck.

She laughed and trailed a finger along my chest, swirling it in little figure eights that were sending shivers down my spine. "You're very good at that." She wrinkled her nose adorably. "Sex, I mean."

"Mmm," I said, as I nibbled on her earlobe.

"Or maybe it's been so long since I got any that I'm just easily impressed."

I grinned against her neck. The little minx. "You were right the first time. I'm very good at that."

She gripped my hair and made me look at her, laughing. "Self esteem is not your problem, is it?"

I shook my head before kissing the tip of her nose. "I had a lot of time after you left, trying to prove to myself that you were just a girl, that what we had was just sexual, that I could find someone better. After you, I made up for my decades being a faithful husband and I went from woman to woman. It wasn't… satisfying, but I learned a few new things."

She frowned at me.

"Oh don't like to hear that I slept around?"

She shook her head with that scowl. Even her scowl was beautiful. I had to laugh.

"Well, having sex with women was never my problem. I'm good at it. I enjoy it. They enjoy it."

Her scowl got thunderous. My jealous little April. It probably didn't say good things about me that I was enjoying her jealousy.

"But it didn't matter how many women I slept with or how good I was in bed, none of them were you. Without you, I had no heart for another woman. So no, April, my problem isn't self esteem. My problem is that you stole my heart and ran away and I've been looking for it ever since."

"Oh." Her voice was small and she ducked her head to hide her face in my neck. I felt hot tears on my skin.

"April?" I rolled her back onto the bed so I could look at her. "What's the matter, darling?"

"I'm so sorry. I'm so sorry. Please, I don't know how you can, but please, forgive me." She covered her face in her hands.

She sobbed in my arms and I gathered her to my chest, but I had nothing to say. I couldn't forgive her.

I loved her. I had missed her. I was happy to have her back, but she had taken my daughter from me. I thought I understood why she ran. I thought I would, someday forgive her, but right now, no matter how much I loved her, I wasn't quite ready yet to forgive.

"I still don't know how I feel about finding out I'm a father. Enraged. Overjoyed. Excited. Sad. I've missed her whole life. It's going to take a while to be able to forgive you, April. Maybe I could forgive you for leaving me, you weren't ready. We went too fast. It's probably my fault. I probably kept pushing the 'keep it light and breezy angle' because I could tell you were scared and I thought I had time to help you be comfortable with me."

"I'm still scared, Charles." The tears were still rolling down her cheeks but the sobs had abated. I wiped them away with my thumb then I kissed her because I had to.

"And I'm still hurt."

She nodded. "What are we going to do?"

I rubbed my hand up and down her arm. She wrapped her arm around my waist and clung to me. "I don't know. I know I want to be Minnie's father. I want to get to know her. I want her to know me as her father."

She swallowed and nodded rapidly. "Yeah. I want that too. I can do that. I-- I don't think it will be too much of a shock. She's always wanted a dad."

"She always had one."

She closed her eyes as a wash of shame flooded over her features. I felt a little guilty at that. I didn't need to make that dig. I didn't want to hurt her.

I didn't want to hurt her.

I didn't want to push her away. No matter how angry I was, I wanted time to get over it, to figure out how I felt. I wasn't going to take it out on her. I needed her to stay with me this time.

"I can bring her over after school if you want. We can break the news to her, then. She likes you, Charles, and she loves Mickey," a slight smile curved her lips. "She'll be happy."

"Today?"

"If you want."

I couldn't keep the laugh from bubbling up. "So soon?"

"I never wanted to deny you your daughter. I was just scared and then more scared and then I was stuck in the lies and guilt and it just spiraled until I couldn't make any choices. I would still be up in the mountains rusticating away if Elisabeth hadn't dragged me back to New York with promises of a brownstone and a store where I could sell my jewelry to rich fools who would pay ridiculous prices for my hippie charms and bracelets."

I was smiling again. She kept making me happy even when I wanted to be mad with her. "Remind me to thank Elisabeth."

"Oh no. Never let her know you owe her something. She'll never let you forget it."

"I don't mind owing her. She brought you back to me. And gave me my daughter. I have a family now."

I saw the moment when panic slipped into her eyes. It was the word 'family.' She blinked and swallowed hard and grew stiff in my arms. I'd pushed too hard. Dammit.

She sat up. "I have to go home."

"Is something wrong?"

She smiled at me, as if her tight, distant smile was

supposed to reassure me. "No, no, nothing at all. I just remembered that I have work to do. I have a big commission coming up for a wedding. Necklaces for all the bridesmaids and tie clips for all the grooms-men. With celadon and amethyst to match the wedding colors." She laughed a fake laugh. "Gotta make the commission, right? You know, you're a businessman." She slid out of bed and grabbed her clothes from the floor, dressing with her back to me.

Dammit.

"April…" I started to say. I didn't want her to go off like this.

"I'll swing by with Minnie after school. Three okay?"

"Yeah, but--"

"Okay." She leaned in and kissed me. I took her hand and held it, I wouldn't let go when she stepped back. "It's okay, Charles. I'm not running, I just have to get some work done."

She was earnest, but radiated a frantic energy. I had to let her go. "All right. Get your work done. I'll see you and Minnie later." I pulled her back in for one more kiss and forced myself to release her. "Can I see you out?"

She laughed lightly, "No, I want to remember you like this." She raked her eyes up my body lasciviously, but wouldn't meet mine.

I let her go.

I heard her running down the stairs, then a few moments of silence, probably finding her bag that she left in the living room, then the front door opened and closed and she was gone.

All I could do was lay there for a moment as I absorbed the revelations of the day. Too many. I was still reeling. And the sheets still smelled of April. Roses and jasmine and a smoky scent that made my toes curl. It was her. She was the one I'd been looking for all these years. And it made no sense, that this woman who had once played with my son as a child could be the woman who made me feel complete.

And yet it was true. I'd done enough searching to know.

I got up and took a shower, getting dressed in my usual clothes. I ate my usual breakfast, if a bit late. I started my day.

But this day had changed my life and none of it felt

the same. I went into my office and went through my emails, and the documents I needed to go over for the next board meeting, but nothing really penetrated. I picked up the acoustic guitar, because learning to play had always been something I'd wanted to do, but I never had time for it until I'd stepped back from my company. But I could only practice for so long before I got itchy. I needed to get up. I needed to do something, to set something to rights. To move.

I knew that nothing felt right because the only thing that mattered was the people I loved. My family. Love was the greatest gift and I'd been given an unexpected bounty in a life that had nearly been erased of all love.

That was why I had quit my job when I had nearly lost Matthew six months ago. Because I wanted to reprioritize my life around the things that mattered. Matthew was still healing from his trials, living out in The Hamptons at the more peaceful beach house, and had resisted my need to bring him back to me, to take care of him.

Of course he had. He was a grown man.

But now I had a daughter. And she was so little, and

so vulnerable and she still had years where she could need a father. I wanted to be that father. And I wanted April. I wanted her now and for the future. I couldn't get the missing years back but I could start on now.

I'd done enough searching in the intervening years. I knew what felt right. April felt right. I wanted to marry her.

But there was no way she was ready for that. Not with the fear I saw leap into her soul when I brought up family. I cursed her father for raising her with the pain of never trusting his love. Family to her was about resentment and deceit and faithlessness and I had underestimated how much that would affect her.

But I could start where I was. I could start now, with the family I had. Matthew. He should know he had a sister.

I put down the guitar with a soft twang from the strings and picked up my phone.

"What's up, Dad? Everything okay?" He picked up, right away and relief swelled through me. It was just good to hear his voice, to know he was safe.

"Yes. I guess. I don't know."

"That doesn't sound good. Do you need me to come back to town?"

"No. No. I just needed to tell you something. It's immense."

"What is it? Are you sick?"

"No. Nothing like that. I don't know how to say it."

"For pete's sake dad, just tell me."

"Fine. I found out, today actually, that you have a sister."

"I have a what?"

That wasn't the right way to tell him. But then, what was the right way? "I found out that my ex-- uh ex girlfriend had a child, and she didn't tell me."

"You-- uh. Wow. Really? Dad, are you sure it's yours? I mean, I hate to say it but you're a rich guy and it could be a con."

"It's not a con." That he would even think April would do such a thing annoyed me. Even if he didn't know it was April yet. "She doesn't need my money.

She wasn't planning on telling me at all. I figured it out."

"How?"

"The eyes."

He was silent for a moment. "The eyes."

"The eyes. My eyes. Same as yours. Your sister has them too."

"My sister. Huh. I have a sister?" I could hear him making noises on the other end that couldn't rightly be translated into words. "I'm coming to Brooklyn. This isn't over the phone news, dad."

"You don't have to. Take care of yourself first."

"I'm coming."

I knew I couldn't stop him. "Wait. There's something else."

"Oh, this has got to be a doozy if you think it's somehow up to 'son you have a sister.'"

"Uh." I suddenly was rethinking telling him. April and I had never told anyone about our relationship. It had been a secret, for valid reasons. But now there was a daughter, and I wasn't keeping that a secret. I wasn't keeping April a secret. "It's about her mother."

"Oh no."

I sighed. "You know her mother."

"I know her? My mind is flipping through all sorts of potential women, dad, you'd better just tell me."

"April."

"Who?"

I rolled my eyes. He knew April. He'd grown up with her. "April Hamilton. From every summer in the Hamptons until you were sixteen or so."

"What? MY April?"

"She's not YOUR April," I snapped. She was mine. I cleared my throat.

"Oh frig dad. You had an affair with April?"

"I did not. There was no affair. We were dating. For a little while. We kept it quiet."

"How is that not an affair? Oh my gosh dad, was she a teenager? Are you that dirty old man?"

"No she wasn't a teenager. She was an adult when we

were seeing each other. Twenty one as a matter of fact. This was a bad idea. I shouldn't have said anything."

"You sure as hell should have. Twenty one. I would have been nineteen. Geez. I haven't seen April since her mom's wedding." He stopped. "Dad did you hook up with April at her mom's wedding?"

That was exactly what I had done. I cleared my throat again. This was more awkward than I'd thought it would be. "Yes, as a matter of fact."

"Well good for you," he said, also awkward. "Good for her, too, I guess. I mean, I'm not going to judge people hooking up even if it's weird for me personally."

"Well thank you." I knew for certain he'd done his own hooking up, in fact I had distinctly remembered some girls sneaking out of my house early in the morning during his college breaks. "But it wasn't exactly a hook up. We kept seeing each other for a while after that until she ran off, actually. She was pregnant already. I didn't know."

"Wait, I remember hearing that she had a kid. Her mom was complaining once and I couldn't get away. That woman has a problem with everything, did you know that? But I thought she was a lesbian. That's right. She wasn't complaining about the kid, she was complaining about the lesbian who wouldn't let her see her granddaughter. Wait. Are you saying the granddaughter is MY SISTER?"

"That would be correct."

"Oh. seriously? April Hamilton is my mom now. I'm never going to let her live it down."

"Don't you dare. I will cut you off."

"No you won't. April is my mom." He started laughing. "This is going to get her back so hard for all the shit she did to me."

"She's not your mom. We're not sure what we are to each other. She ran away the first time. I don't want to scare her away again. If you freak her out I will banish you to The Hamptons and you will regret ever saying a word."

"Wait. You're serious. Oh. Wait, are you serious about April? Are you in love with her?"

"Matthew, that's not something I particularly want to talk about with you."

"Holy shit you are. You're in love with April Hamilton. How old is this kid? What is her name? I have a sister. Holy shit."

"Her name is Minnie. Minerva. She's going to be seven next week."

"I have a sister." It was different this time he said it. I couldn't really get a read on his feelings.

"Matthew."

"I'll be there this afternoon."

"No, you don't need to--" But it was already too late. He'd hung up. I knew there was nothing I could do to make him not come. When he set his mind to something, he let nothing get in his way. Not me. Not storms. Not the sea itself.

I admired that about him. He wasn't bound by what was expected of him, or social rules. Or duty. Not like I was. April had the right of it. I'd married his mother out of duty and stayed with her because of it, too. And I would have married April out of duty also.

Maybe she was right. Maybe I would have begun to hate her. Maybe I would have resented being trapped in another accidental pregnancy marriage.

But she wasn't pregnant now. And I still wanted her, desperately. Wanted to keep her. Wanted to love her and wanted her to love me.

I'd taken my time and seen what else was out there and nothing, nothing at all, ever compared to April or how she made me feel. It wasn't a fling. It wasn't an affair. It was love and it was special and I wasn't going to let her run away from me again because she was scared.

Was I supposed to wait for her to decide she wasn't afraid of what it meant to be with me anymore? Was I supposed to tip toe around how I felt and not be who I wanted to be to her and to my daughter? No. I wasn't going to.

This wasn't duty anymore.

I grabbed my keys and wallet and left, without thinking about it, walking directly towards Elisabeth's so called "bohemian emporium."

It was in a building with four floors, but the first two floors were taken up with storefronts. A few steps down led you to the restaurant. It had not opened yet and I could see lots of work being done inside. Up the wrought iron stairs, there was a second storefront, a bay window bumping out above the first floor. I walked up to the second floor and opened the door to the yoga studio.

Mona was standing at the counter, going over some papers. "Oh!" she said.

"Mona, is she here?"

"I, uh, I don't know." She knew. Her eyes were very wide, waiting to see what I would do next. She might know everything that had happened, actually. I bet April told her everything.

"I need to talk to her. I'm not mad. I just need to see her."

"Why?"

So this was all coming out into the open was it? Good. It never should have been a secret. Maybe if it hadn't been before April wouldn't have felt the need to keep her pregnancy a secret and we could have had a life together. But we could fix that now. "Because I love her, and I don't want to do what I did last time and let her get away."

Her face remained impassive but she nodded. "She's up the stairs. First door on your left."

"Thank you." I turned to go.

"You'll need the keys."

When I turned back around she dangled a set with a tye dyed teddy bear attached to them. "You're giving me your keys? Why?"

"Because I'm the one that convinced her to run away when she found out she was pregnant, and it's torn her up so badly I regret it every day. And I am sorry you never got to know Minnie. She's a great kid. I love her." Tears had come to her eyes although her face still remained like stone. "I need to apologize for my part in what happened. And I need to make amends."

I took the keys. "Did you and Elisabeth know I lived in this neighborhood when you brought April and Minnie to live here?"

She pressed her lips into a thin line. "Mmm. Might have done."

"Do you two ever not get your way?"

She shrugged, but a tiny smile sneaked its way onto her face.

As I left I spotted the shop cases by the bay window, lit with sparkling lights, the silver jewelry inside seemed alive. Rings and necklaces and bracelets cunningly designed to give the impression of nature--leaves, flowers, grasses, twigs all wrought in silver and studded with semi precious stones. There seemed to be the suggestion of tiny creatures hiding in the foliage and they almost seemed to sway in the breeze.

"Is this her work?"

"Yes. She's very talented, isn't she?"

I was stunned. It was magical.

"We are all very protective of her and we won't let anyone hurt her."

"Neither will I, I promise."

"Good. Welcome to the family, Beau. Give her time, she'll come around."

I nodded and headed upstairs.

CHAPTER THIRTEEN: APRIL

$\mathcal{I}$ was good at avoiding things I didn't want to think about. I had years, if not decades, of practice at it. I ran home from Charles' place and took a shower, changing into my most comfortable and oldest jeans and tshirt, filled with holes because I couldn't give up the soft fabric and the memories from the festival I'd attended in college. And then I put on my headphones so I could get in the mood and turned on music that was far distant from this place and time. The kind Mona's parents used to play. I sat down at my jewelry bench and began filing the jewelry I had due.

I hadn't lied. I really did have to finish the order, but I had fibbed a bit. I was ahead. And had plenty of time to finish it. But I couldn't worry about that right now. All I needed to do was focus on the next step at hand, the next tie pin, the next necklace, the next ring.

'Landslide' by Fleetwood Mac came on and I sang along, filing and shaping, oh I knew what it was like for the landslide to come along. Right now the ground had been swept out from under my feet and I was brought down.

A touch at my elbow had me jump. I dropped the tie pin and the file. "Dammit, Mona--" I turned to scold her.

It wasn't Mona.

Charles stood there, a shy smile on his face. Shy? I took off my headphones and turned off the music.

"That's the best song. Your voice is lovely. I can't believe I've never heard you sing before."

"What are you doing here?"

"I'm sorry, I didn't mean to interrupt your work."

My work at keeping myself from freaking out about my feelings for Charles? Well that was donc. My heart was racing a mile a minute and yet I was glad to see him.

I raised my eyebrows and put down my supplies, twirling on the stool to face him.

"Clearly I did anyway, but I just didn't want to leave things between us the way we did."

Of course he didn't. I'd taken his daughter from him and he had no guarantee I wouldn't run off again. "Don't worry, Charles. I will make sure you have a good relationship with Minnie from now on. I mean as much as we can. We can plan days where you can take her. Maybe we can trade off where she sleeps? Or who picks her up after school. Or weekends. I can give you weekends." The thought of no longer having Minnie with me all the time was a cut to my soul. But he deserved weekends with her, too. "No matter what happens between us, I trust you with her, I do."

I thought he'd be happy. I thought that was what he wanted, but his face got more and more troubled, ending with his lips compressed into a tight line and his nostrils flaring as he shook his head slowly.

"That is exactly what I'm talking about."

"What? You want primary custody?" The fear leapt again. He wouldn't do that to me. Would he?

"No! I would never take her from you." The relief swept through me but he wasn't done. "Of course I want to be her father and get to know her, but I think you're confused."

"Oh most definitely. I'm confused about everything. I'm just muddling through this whole thing I've been terrified of for years."

He growled quietly in the back of his throat and a thrill went through me. Dammit. I would never not respond physically to him. He looked around my studio which was cluttered, but I sometimes used to meet with clients. There was a small seating area with low chairs. "Can we talk for a minute?" He took my hand before I answered, but once I felt his skin against mine, there was no other answer I could give him but yes. He led me to the chairs, had me sit then pulled the other closer to mine and sat opposite me, so he could keep holding my hand.

"April. I want to be in Minnie's life, yes. But what I'm talking about right now is us. I need to be clear about what I want with us."

I was suddenly thirsty and my mouth was dry, but my water bottle was sitting on the jewelry bench and

I couldn't at all break contact with his pale green eyes, or let go of his hand that was keeping me from floating off into the ether. "What do you want with us?" The words were a whisper that barely came out of my mouth.

He cocked his head and gave me a warm smile. "I want to be with you. I want everyone to know that I love you. I want to go to sleep with you in my arms every night, and I want to wake up to your face being the first thing I see every morning. I want you."

I could not breathe with the longing lodged firmly in my chest. "But we can't. There's too much at risk. What if my mother won't accept us."

"I'm not asking for her permission. I have never asked for her approval in my life before." Of course he hadn't. But I had. "And if she doesn't accept your choice, then I'll be here for you. I'll protect you. I'll support you. And we'll make our family our own way."

That word again. Family. I remembered how my father disappeared every weekend on retreats and conventions and business meetings, but we all knew he was leaving to spend time with the wife and child he really loved.

It was like Charles could read my mind. "I'm not your father, April. I won't do what he did."

"But you married your wife--"

"It doesn't matter that I married my wife and never loved her."

"Charles!" I was shocked.

"I mean of course it matters, but I've done a lot of soul searching since you've been gone, wondering what I wanted in life, what I wanted from love, and though I spent a lot of time not believing that I needed love, when Matthew was lost at sea when his plane went down, I realized that love was what mattered most. Love is the greatest gift."

I gasped. "Matthew was lost at sea? His plane went down?"

"Oh. I didn't get a chance to tell you that, did I? Yes. About six months ago. He was found by a small sail-boat after two days of floating in the ocean. He's still recovering, and so am I. I stepped back from my business and went to therapy. I've been facing my history as a not great husband or father. I know what I want now and how I want to live my life, what is important." He grasped my hand in both of his. My stomach flipped.

"Charles…"

"I want you. And Minnie. I want love, and a real family. An honest one, one that doesn't spin off into opposite directions of the globe, but is centered and strengthened by their connections. Will you be that for me?"

I wanted it. I wanted it so much. "But what if what we have isn't real? What if we realize down the line that it was just sex or attraction or the thrill of a secret affair and the scandal of it all."

"Oh, April," he said and pulled me to sit in his lap. "Do you really think that's true? After almost eight years apart and these feelings that are stronger than ever? Do you think actually spending time together would make it fade?"

I shrugged. "Maybe. And I can't take that chance because now it's not just my heart and yours at risk of being broken, it's Minnie's."

I wanted him to understand how important that was. How essential.

He nodded and twisted a lock of hair that had fallen from my bun to stick it behind my ear. "Yes, you're right. But I'm that sure of us. I know we're meant to be together."

"You can't know."

"I do, but you don't. So I'm willing to date you instead of marrying you at the courthouse this week."

I gasped. "Charles! Don't joke."

He chuckled throatily. "You think I'm joking? I want to marry you. I want to do it seven years ago, but next week will suffice."

I opened my mouth to tell him how that was impossible but he put a finger to my lips to silence me.

"But I know you're not ready. We can date. As adults, getting to know each other again. And we can go out as a family with Minnie, but keep that non-romantic if you want... although that will be hard for me to keep from touching you."

"Charles!" I wanted to scold him but had a hard time pushing my amusement away.

"And I can have dates with my daughter without you, and you can figure out what you need as a woman and individual. And I can introduce her to her brother--"

"Oh Matthew." I had never forgotten him. How could I? My old friend whose father I fell in love with, whose sister I had given birth to.

"Yes, Matthew. It turns out I told him about his sister. And you."

"You didn't!"

I won't keep you secret again. I won't. I'm not ashamed of you or us or Minnie. This is for real and everyone should know I love you."

"Not Minnie!"

"Not Minnie yet. But it's going to be obvious to her sooner rather than later. If she's anything like you were as a kid. You were extraordinarily bright."

"This is all so scary. It's so important and so risky."

"Everything worth having is. Take a risk on us, April."

I wanted to say yes. But I couldn't, not yet.

"You can keep your life here. I'll keep my life in my house and we'll just agree to meet in the middle. Say... the dog park?"

I slapped at his chest, feeling joy rise in mine. I wanted to laugh. I wanted to be happy. I wanted to love. I wanted to be with him. "Okay," I said half reluctant, half ecstatic. "We can meet at the dog park. Minnie will be happy."

"So you're my girlfriend."

"Casual girlfriend," I emphasized. "Who sleeps over when she has a babysitter." I didn't know if he remembered that I lived with my babysitters, but I wasn't going to tell him.

"Casual girlfriend who sleeps over it is."

Casual I could do. Then a thought occurred to me. He'd been casual with women all over town for the last seven years. "But no other women!" The words came out like a demand.

He raised one eyebrow. "Okay. No other women. Not a problem at all. I only want you. We'll date exclusively but casually while making love at every opportunity and raising a daughter together platonically."

It sounded completely contradictory and I was okay with that. He was restraining a grin. "Yes. Now get out of here so I can finish my work. I'll see you when I bring Minnie by after school." I jumped off his lap and he let me go.

"I'll see you then." He looked entirely too pleased with himself as he let himself out the door.

"Hey!"

He turned around. "Did you have some other stipulation to our relationship?"

I grabbed his collar and pulled him in for a kiss full of relief and happiness. When the kiss ended he could barely open his eyes.

"Yes. The stipulation that if Minnie is not around, you're never allowed to leave without kissing me goodbye."

Eyes still closed, he smiled. "I like that stipulation."

"Good. Now go." I pushed him out the door as he laughed.

⁓

I TOLD MINNIE THAT CHARLES WAS HER FATHER ON the walk over to his house. For some reason, I didn't want to spring it on her in front of him. Maybe I wanted to give her a chance to react or process without hurting his feelings. Maybe I wanted to be able to comfort her first.

But she didn't need comfort. She barely responded. "Okay," she'd said and just kept walking, quiet, which was unlike her on a Friday afternoon, but I decided to let her process it in silence if she needed to.

That's when the text came.

old man: you unblocked my number

me: I did that 7 years ago. I thought you might call but you never did.

old man: I was trying to respect your wishes. my phone calls you 'chippie.' I want to keep it for nostalgia.

old man: You're old man on my phone.

I smiled at the thought, then looked at Minnie to make sure she was okay. She was still staring off into space.

me: I told Minnie you're her dad. I didn't want to freak her out.

old man: Is she taking it okay?

me: not sure yet. but we're almost to your house.

old man: I'm glad. But you should be aware that Matthew just showed up to meet his sister. I told him to stay upstairs until she's ready. He promised.

I sighed. This was going to be a very big day and I hoped it wouldn't be too much for her.

old man: if she's not ready, we just won't introduce him today. we'll save it for another day.

We were on the Promenade with the cool breeze from the river and the silvery skyline of Manhattan on the other side. Minnie's attention was caught by the city, and she still hadn't said anything. But here we were. And we might as well get this over with.

me: we're here.

I laid Minnie up the stairs and by the time we got to the top, Charles was opening the door.

"Hi Minnie Mouse."

She looked up at him, her face scrunched up in a question.

"Why don't you come in?"

"Thanks," she said and went in as he held the door for her. "Mickey!" she cried, as soon as she saw the dog, animated again at last.

Charles leaned in, sneaking a kiss on my cheek, and whispered. "It'll be fine."

"You don't know that."

"I do, because whatever happens, we'll deal with it."

He led us all to the living room where the coffee table was spread with a platter of rainbow colored petit fours, small glasses and a pitcher of lemonade.

"You made us a tea party?"

Minnie's eyes got wide. "Mama can I have the cakes?"

"Go ahead, but not too many. You made her cakes?"

Charles laughed. "No. My housekeeper did. She's excited to have a young lady about the house. She did one in every color because she wasn't sure what color would be Minnie's favorite."

Minnie looked up with a small blue cake in her hand and an orange one going into her mouth. "I like all the colors, so she did excellent." She grinned and I could breathe again.

"I will tell her."

She stopped before popping the blue one in her mouth. "Are you really my father?"

"I am. Is that okay with you?"

"Hmm," she said. "Does that mean that Mickey is my dog?"

"I suppose it does. I will keep him here though, so you can see him when you're here, or when we go for walks. Would you like to sit down?"

She shook her head and ate the blue cake, reaching for the lemonade.

"Let me." Charles poured her a glass then poured one for me, offering it with a smile. "Please sit, April. Get comfortable."

I sat and sipped at the lovely lemonade and watched my daughter sort through the cakes, bringing me a purple one, since she knew that was my favorite color.

Charles called Mickey to his side and then sat on the couch next to me. Minnie didn't even notice. She was too busy coveting all the cakes. "Only one more, Minnie."

She frowned at me. "Three more."

"Two."

She nodded without protest before grabbing a pink one and another purple one and then climbing up into Charles' lap.

He blinked. Stunned.

"Can I call you daddy?"

He nodded. I could see his throat swallowing before he choked out a "yes," and then put his arm around her shoulders.

She ate one cake and then asked for her lemonade, and Charles handed it to her, at her beck and command, I thought. She could ask for anything and he'd give it to her. Because he was like that.

My heart softened watching them.

"Do you like movies, daddy?"

"I've never really had the opportunity to watch a lot

of movies, I was always working too much. But I don't do that anymore, so maybe you could tell me which ones I should watch."

Minnie's eyes lit up as she told him about all her favorite movies, only occasionally including me in the conversation. From then, they moved on to food, and then of course dogs, and he told her about the ocean, which she'd never been to. That had totally been my fault, hiding away in the mountains and refusing to see my family on the coast. He promised to take her there. And I began thinking of holidays in East Hampton, spending the summers at the beach, with Minnie and Charles and maybe Mona and Elisabeth coming up when they had time, and... it sounded like a life I wanted to live.

The housekeeper, Mrs. Edwards came in and Charles had her bring some coffee for us, almond milk in mine. His phone beeped while Minnie was chattering away on his lap, this time about her grandma and grandpa in the mountains. He peeked and then held it up for me to see.

Matt: Can I come down and meet my sister yet?

I took a deep breath. "Minnie, honey. There's something else." She looked up, entirely happy and pleased from Charles' lap. "Charles has a son. That makes him your brother."

"I have a brother? Can I play with him?"

"Probably," Charles said, "But he's a lot older than you, he's closer to your mom's age. He's not a kid. He might be more like an uncle."

"Maybe he should marry Momo."

I choked on my coffee. "No, I don't think that's likely, honey. He's not her type at all."

"Lissie?"

"He doesn't have to marry anyone. He's still your family. And so are Momo and Lissie."

"He can come to my birthday party and bring me a present."

"Minnie!" How was she so mercenary? I hadn't taught her that.

"It's a deal, what would you like for your birthday? I hear you're seven." Matthew stood in the doorway, his blonde hair tousled and a grin on his face. Minnie jumped up from Charles' lap and came to stand in front of him. He squatted down. "I'm Matthew," he said, holding out his hand for her to shake. "Hello, sis."

"I'm Minerva. You can call me Minnie." She peered at him then looked back at Charles. "We all have the same color eyes."

"So we do." Matthew winked at me. "I guess that means we're family."

CHAPTER FOURTEEN: CHARLES

I was sitting on the bench in the dog park with Mickey bright and early, waiting for Minnie and April, sipping my coffee, when Mickey perked up. His tail started wagging and he could barely keep seated. I knew they were here and I made myself wait, anticipating seeing them again, until I looked up.

When I finally did, April was opening the gate, watching me as I pretended to be cool. She looked amused. The sight of her and my daughter made my chest fill with happiness, like an ocean breeze or birds singing or something that poets wrote about.

"Daddy!" Minnie cried and came running, throwing herself into my arms. I hugged her, treasuring her slight weight. She actually greeted me before the dog. Who was now leaping about us, overjoyed.

"Hey sweetheart, did you have a good sleep?" She nodded, but then pushed to get down so she could greet Mickey. I didn't mind. I wanted her to be happy.

I smiled at her outfit, a sundress in her favorite color: all of them, green leggings with black and white panda bears, and pink sneakers. Her hair was done up in pigtails again. She wasn't wearing her sunglasses. "I like to see your eyes. They're very pretty."

"Thanks, daddy, I like your eyes too." She grinned like she wanted to say more, but Mickey wanted her to throw a stick and chase him, and these were the important things to an almost seven year old. "Can I put the leash on him? I want to practice walking him."

"Of course," I said, fastening the leash to his collar and watched her go, leading him around the dog park, a grin I could not stop spreading across my face.

April sat down next to me with a groan. "Ugh. It's Saturday. Did we have to walk Mickey this early?"

I shot her a look and my grin broke into a smile. She'd left her hair loose and curling like she knew I liked, and was wearing a pretty floral sundress and bare sandals. She had dressed up for me. And her frown was as fake as her complaint, the corners of her mouth sneaking up into a smile. I snuck a peak to make sure Minnie was distracted and then kissed her swiftly on the lips.

"Morning, darling."

"Charles…" she scolded, swatting me playfully, but then she settled in next to me, handing me a cup from a paper bag she carried. "Here, this is for you." She popped a straw in the top.

"What is this? It's not coffee." It was green. Bright green.

"It's a green smoothie. It's good for you."

I eyed it suspiciously. "It doesn't look good for me. It looks vile for me."

"Try it. It's good. It's full of fruit."

"Then why is it green?"

She rolled her eyes. "You have to try it. You're in love with me and this is the honeymoon period."

"Oh ho, is that how we're playing this? Using my infatuation with you to get me to do what you want?"

She smirked. "If I have to. Besides I want to take care of you. I'm in love with you, too."

My heart flipped. "It's hard to argue with that." I worked up my nerve and took a sip while she watched expectantly. "Okay, it's pretty decent. It tastes good. In fact I feel better already."

"Good." Then she reached across me and stole my coffee from the bench where it had been sitting. "Hey! Thief."

She grinned as she drank. "You love me. You have to give me your coffee."

"Yeah, okay. You got me there, darling." I laughed and shook my head, putting my arm around her shoulders and pulling her to my side. It felt so good to have her there. "You know, I missed you last night."

She nodded slowly. "I missed you, too. So did Minnie. She wanted you to put her to bed."

I inhaled deeply. That sounded wonderful.

"Maybe tonight, you could come over and I could make you dinner and we could spend some family time, and then you could put her to bed."

"I would like that." It sounded wonderful. I played with her hair, curling a silky lock around my finger. "And then after she goes to bed, can I put you to bed, too?"

She didn't answer, not even to tease or scold. A soft breath left her lips that I might not even have noticed if I weren't paying such close attention. She wanted it, too. But she was afraid to want it.

I withdrew my arm. "Don't worry, I'm not going to push you. I can wait until you're ready."

She grabbed my hand. "No that's not it. I am ready. I've been ready for you for years. I've been waiting when I thought I never had a chance to have you back. It just doesn't seem real. It doesn't seem like I can have Minnie, and…" Her brown eyes were large and sincere. I brushed a strand of hair back from her cheek just to have an excuse to touch her. "Love," she sighed. "I thought it was all in my head. A fantasy. But here you are and you're real and it's hard to reconcile that. Hard to believe."

"I'm real, darling. I'm here." I held tight to her

fingers. "I'm not the dream you imagined. I'm not perfect. It's probably my fault my first marriage never amounted to anything. I blamed her for trapping me, and didn't think about her needs, and refused to make any compromises for our family. I have a lot of regrets in my life, not the least is letting you go seven years ago. I should have fought for you. I should have made Elisabeth tell me where you were. But you'd rejected me so I didn't. I focused on my 'purpose' instead until I found out that my purpose was worth nothing if I didn't have love. I'm proud, and rather stodgy and boring. All work and no play. I'm trying to change that, trying to be that man that you made me think I could be seven years ago. I'm starting with loving you and Minnie, and learning to listen to your needs. So if you want to take it slow, that's what I'll do. But I still want you to know that I thought about you all night. Your skin, your hair, that sigh you make."

She sighed.

"Yes that one."

She grinned at me. "You think you're stodgy and boring but you make me feel safe and protected."

I made a face. "Safe and protected. Am I a bank?"

"No, you're a glorious man. With a single glance of your eyes, I melt. And it's okay if I melt, because you're there to take care of me and make sure I'm okay until I can gather my wits again."

"Well, then, that's okay." I saw her looking at my lips, like she wanted to kiss me. I thought I'd let her make the first move this time. I wouldn't push.

She looked around to see if Minnie was paying attention and then suddenly sat upright. "Where is she?"

The dog park had plenty of people with their dogs, but no Minnie. No Mickey, either.

I stood. "Minnie!" She stood, too.

"Minnie!" She went around to all the benches and trees looking behind to see if they were playing hide and seek. I checked with the other dog walkers. None of them had seen Minnie. How could a little girl just disappear.

April came back to my side, her eyes wild with panic. "Charles they're not here. Oh my gosh. Where is Minnie?"

"Don't panic. We'll find her."

"Don't panic? My daughter is missing! Oh my god. Oh my god. While we were making googly eyes at each other she vanished. Was she kidnapped? You're a billionaire, what if they want a ransom."

"Shh." I took her by the shoulders and rubbed my hands up and down her arms. "No one even knows I'm her father. I'm sure she just wandered off. She took Mickey with her. No one would kidnap a child and a dog."

"Mickey's with her." She took in a gasping breath of air. "He won't let anyone hurt her."

"We're going to go find her." He grabbed her bag from the bench and tossed all the drinks in the trash. "Let's go."

He held onto her hand, she seemed to need the support and went for the gate.

"Is it closed? I think I left the gate open when we came in. Why was I so careless? It's my fault."

"No," he said as they passed through. "She's almost seven and she's been working out how to open that gate for two weeks. I'm sure she just figured it out. She said she wanted to practice walking Mickey. She didn't mean inside the dog park. Dammit."

She stood on the sidewalk outside of the dog park with her hands cupped around her mouth. "Minnie!"

"Maybe she went home. Call Mona. I'll call Matthew in case Mickey takes her to my house. He's very stubborn on the leash."

"Matthew," I said, no time for pleasantries. "Is Minnie there?"

"No, of course not."

"No Mickey, either?"

"No, what's going on. I thought you took him for a walk."

"I did, and I met Minnie and April at the dog park. Minnie and the dog went missing from the dog park."

Matthew's tone sharpened. "When?"

"Couldn't have been more than ten or fifteen minutes ago."

"I'll be at the dog park in five minutes."

"No. Go to the smoothie place. Check all the little stores on the street that might draw an almost seven year old. Call me if you find them."

"Got it." The phone clicked off.

April turned to me. "She's not at home. Mona is going to check the yoga studio and the restaurant."

"Matthew's going to the smoothie place to see if she's there."

"Oh that's good. That's good." She wiped at her eyes and I couldn't bear to see her so heartbroken. I pulled her into a hug.

"Where else might she go? What did she like to do with you?"

She shrugged and looked up. "The playground?"

"Good that's where we should go." I took her hand again and we walked down the street. We'd only gone a couple of blocks when we came upon a couple fighting. No, not a couple.

Elisabeth and Jack.

April hurtled full force into Elisabeth's arms, crying. "Minnie's gone, Lissie. She wandered off from the dog park with Mickey and now we don't know where she was. Oh Lissie I'm a terrible mother. I lost my daughter."

Elisabeth's face drained of blood and she looked to me for confirmation. I nodded. "When?"

"Fifteen minutes ago," April sobbed. Elisabeth took a cotton handkerchief out of her pocket and wiped her tears.

Duke who had just been standing there watching the women cling to each other, raked a hand through his too long black hair. "It's that big shaggy dog, right?" He turned to me.

I nodded. "Goldendoodle. Named Mickey."

"Little girl is about yay high," he held his hand up, "with brown hair like hers and green eyes like…" He stopped and cocked his head. "Like yours actually."

I ground my teeth. "She's my daughter."

He nodded but didn't say anything. "How far can a little girl and a dog go in fifteen minutes?"

"I don't know. A few blocks. He might be pulling on the leash and she might have to run to keep up."

He nodded. "Got it. I'll put out an alert with the neighborhood."

"Duke!" Elisabeth yelled as he walked away. "Where are you going? We need help."

"Gonna ride the perimeter. See how far a little girl and a dog could go." He got on a motorcycle parked on the street.

"Oh thank you duke. Do you need my number to call if you find her."

"I'll call the princess." With that he revved his motor-cycle and raced off.

"Princess?" I asked.

"He means me," Elisabeth said. "Wait. I just had a thought. Your mother." She pointed at April.

"What about my mother? I cannot deal with her right now."

"Your mother has been complaining about how you're denying her her granddaughter for years now. She hates Mona, by the way."

"I know. Get to the point."

"What if your mom, like, decided to stop waiting and decided to meet Minnie on her own."

"You're saying my mom kidnapped Minnie?" April scoffed and looked at me.

"Actually, maybe. She never stops talking about

Mona stole her daughter and her granddaughter from her and I haven't talked to her since you've been back in New York, but it must be driving her insane that you're in the same city as she is and she still hasn't seen her."

April clutched at me. "Call her. Call her please. I can't-- I can't deal with her right now, and I don't think she would do that, it's too scandalous, but please call her to make sure."

Anything. I would do anything. I found her number in my contacts and rang her.

"Why hello, Beau," her cultured voice rang in my ear. "To what do I owe the pleasure of your call? We were just getting ready to head out to The Hamptons and I was wondering if we'd see you there."

"Barbara, I don't mean to be rude, but we're having a bit of an emergency that I'm hoping you could help me with."

"Of course, Beau. How can I be of service?"

"Did you come to Brooklyn to meet your grand-daughter, Minnie?"

There was no answer for four heartbeats. I counted. My heartbeats were loud. "I most certainly did not."

I closed my eyes in disappointment. It had been a long shot.

"Why? And why are you, of all people, making this call?"

"Because Minnie is missing, and as it turns out, I am Minnie's father."

"Charles!" April dug her fingernails into my arm. "What are you saying?"

"I'm not keeping Minnie a secret, April. She's mine. I'm not keeping you a secret either. No more secrets."

"Let me talk to my daughter."

"There's no time. We're searching for Minnie. We just needed to check with you. Thank you, we can talk later."

I hung up while she was still sputtering.

April's eyes were huge and filled with tears. "It's my fault, Charles."

I pulled her to me and wrapped her in my arms as if I could protect her from the world. I knew I could not. "Don't lose hope. We'll find her. We're setting everyone to looking. Stay with me, okay? We'll find her."

She took a deep breath and nodded. "It's not the time to fall apart. We'll find her."

"Elisabeth, could you check the playground and the school for us? I will take her home so we can be there if Minnie shows up, and we'll call the police. They'll probably want documents and photos."

April closed her eyes but nodded. "Yes. We have to call the police now. Just to be safe."

Elisabeth reached out and held her hand. "We'll find her, I swear."

We parted ways, Elisabeth to the playground and April and I back to her house. We would find her.

CHAPTER FIFTEEN: APRIL

*C*harles and I met Mona at home. She opened the door and handed me a cup of herbal tea before I even got in.

"For your nerves," she said as she patted my back. "We'll find her. I know we will."

I nodded and sipped the tea, which was actually more helpful than I thought it would be. She went out to check all the places Minnie usually loved, and Charles called the police, which I appreciated. I was too shaken to talk to anyone, and he was organized and in control and took care of everything. I was so grateful that he could tell me what to do next because my brain was still in panic mode. He told me what the police needed from me and I rounded up all the documentation that they asked for. It was horrifically businesslike.

In no time at all, the police were at my door asking for all sorts of things that they could use to track her down. When they asked what she was wearing, I blanked. "Leggings and a dress...I don't remember." How could I forget what my own daughter was wearing? "I'm the worst mother in the world." A sob broke free from my throat, and Charles bundled me into his arms.

"I remember." He spoke over my head while I cried into his chest, finally having my breakdown. "She was wearing a sundress in her favorite color: all of them."

I looked up at him, he was pale and grim, but he was focused and his presence steadied me. "That's right. That's one of her favorites." I could remember now. "It's, uhm, in tiers? Red, orange, blue, green, going from top to bottom."

He nodded, a small smile on his lips. "And green leggings with black and white panda bears, and pink sneakers. Her hair was done up in pigtails."

"Two." I nodded. He'd been paying attention. He held me tight. This was my biggest nightmare, but he made me believe things would be okay if I could just hold on. So I clung to him even tighter.

"We'll find her, darling. This is just a precaution. Mickey is with her. I'm sure she just went off on a practice walk like she said."

"She's not allowed to go out alone. It's dangerous."

"It is. You're right. And she's too young to be out there alone, but kids break rules. Some more than others. You want to keep them safe and you do your best, but ultimately, it's up to them. The older they get, the harder it is to keep them safe. Matthew was a daredevil, always going off on the most heart stopping adventures. I don't know where he got it from. But in the end, even when it seemed like all was lost, he came home, safe."

He spoke sense. I knew he spoke sense. I'd been that adventurous child once and I'd led Matthew on some of his adventures, but I'd calmed down as I got older and Minnie-- Minnie was too young.

The policeman took my contact number and all the documents and written details we could remember and told us he would send out an alert for her with the rest of the officers. They would all be on the lookout and be in contact with us. He left and Charles and I were alone.

"If we'd been in the mountains and Minnie wandered away from me, it wouldn't be a thing at all. She'd come back later with a collection of stones and mud all over her dress."

"Or she'd be lost in the wilderness with the wild animals and I'd have to call in the helicopters."

"You wouldn't."

"Oh wouldn't I? The only thing that's keeping me from doing it now is that helicopters would not help at all in Brooklyn Heights. But we're doing what we can. Searching. Getting help from friends and neigh-bors. Bringing the police in." He hugged me. I could feel his heart beating, strong and steady. If it weren't for him I would be panicking completely. "She'll come back from this too, with dog drool all over her dress. Don't worry."

"How can you say not to worry, Charles. My daugh-ter-- our daughter is lost in New York City."

"She's wandering. That's not the same as lost."

"Anything could happen. Someone could snatch her!"

"No one is going to snatch her with that giant dog at her side. He may be silly but he makes her less of a target to anyone looking for an easy target, okay? Dogs were made to keep children safe."

"No. That's true, you're right."

"Now everyone in the neighborhood is out looking for her and the police will start a door to door search soon."

I fell into the soft cushions of the yellow sofa. "Half an hour ago, everything in life was beautiful. I had hope. But because I was selfish and careless, I let it all fall apart."

"Oh, April," he said, and sat next to me. "You have to have faith. It's too soon to lose hope. I know you're scared, but the chances are she just wandered away with the dog and if that's so, someone will find her or she'll wander back soon."

"It's my fault. I wasn't paying attention."

"For five minutes, darling. In a closed park within earshot. You can't keep her tied to you for her whole life. Children do things they shouldn't, they wander off. And then you're there for them when things need to be fixed. You've got to stop blaming yourself for everything."

"Easier said than done. And every time, it's about you."

"Me?"

"I was afraid to let myself have you seven years ago so I ran away. And now I thought I'd have a chance to have you and I lost my daughter."

"No. That wasn't it. It wasn't because we had a chance to be together, or even because we were talking instead of watching her. You can have me and she will be safe."

"How do you know?"

"Because I believe."

"Believe in what? That nothing bad can happen? That's patently untrue. Happy endings aren't how life really works."

"No. Happy endings can happen. Of course bad things happen all the time, but I believe that good things can happen too, and we don't have to pay for them with suffering. And when bad things happen, we deal with them." He stood up and held his hand out to me. "Come on. We're going to go look for her now. She'll be getting an ice cream or playing happily with Mickey."

I sighed and wiped the tears. "We're going to find her and she'll be fine. She just wandered away." I didn't believe it really, I still couldn't believe in happy endings, but I believed in Charles, and he believed. I didn't know why.

We checked to make sure we had all the information we needed and plenty of photos to identify her to the neighborhood storekeepers as we got ready for our search.

He led me outside and I was stunned that the day could be so lovely. How dare it be summer sweet today when my world was falling apart? The sky was blue with high puffy clouds and the temperature was perfect. The trees lining the city sidewalks were in full leaf, and casting cool green shadows on the pedestrians who strolled here and there. How was it possible that the world had kept turning despite Minnie going missing?

We were just at the bottom of the stoop when my phone rang. My heart leapt into my throat. It was Elisabeth. "What is it Lissie? Did you find her?"

Charles clutched my elbow. He was worried too, no matter how he tried to stay calm for me, I knew.

"No. I didn't." Disappointed I shook my head so Charles would know. He released his hold on my arm. "But, someone did see her walking down the street with Mickey. An old lady walking her miniature poodle near the Promenade. She thought it was inappropriate that a child should be walking such a large dog. Wasn't she in that dress that looked like a half a rainbow today?"

"Yes!"

"Then it was definitely her. The lady didn't like her dress, either."

I gasped. "Someone saw her by the river!" Charles went alert.

Elisabeth continued. "I called Duke to ride down there on his motorcycle because he can get there first. And I'm heading out there, too, so if she's on her way back I'll run into her. I'll call Mona to come in from the other direction, so one of us is bound to find her."

I nodded, my mouth dry before I remembered she

was on the phone and couldn't see me. "Yes. Yes. Do that."

"That's by my house," Charles said thumbing his phone. "I'll tell Matthew to go back and watch for them on the stoop incase Mickey leads her back there."

I told Elisabeth about Matthew at Charles' house, another spot to find her. And just in case, I'd have the shop girl at the yoga studio keep her eye out for her here. "Oh my god, she's going to be okay," I breathed.

"She is. We'll find her," Lissie said and then as soon as she hung up I found myself crying.

Charles pulled me into his chest. "You were right, Charles. You were right. I just needed to believe."

"And have people who love you and are there for you, April. We're here for you. We won't let you down."

I called the police and told them the new information and Charles called Matthew, and just after we put the yoga studio girls on the lookout, and we started to head down towards the Promenade, a crowd of sleek black cars pulled up at the curb in front of us.

"What the?" It was intimidating, these expensive almost official looking cars. "Did you do this Charles? Call some sort of black ops people?"

He shook his head, looking puzzled at first, then he blinked. "Oh. Oh April. You called your mother."

"What? No," then I stared in horror as the door opened and my mother and aunt Donna came rushing out of one of the sleek black cars.

"April!" my mother cried and walked up to me.

"Mother." I said, not knowing what to do. "We don't have time. Someone sighted Minnie, I have to go."

"Oh, my daughter," she said, and before I could explain or defend myself or step back, she hugged me. "I'm so sorry." she said, holding tight to my arms as if I'd run away. I was thinking of it. "For everything. We're here to help." Aunt Donna came in, too and joined us both in her hug.

"We missed you April," she said. "Welcome home."

That's when I noticed that the other doors were

opening up. Grandmother was there, being helped out of her car by her driver, chic as ever in her silver white chignon and a long tunic of linen. I winced, because she was carrying a glossy black cane, and my grandmother had never needed a cane before. She was getting old and I missed it. Then came my step father Joe. Even my brother Jack, who I'd barely talked to before I left home. He was older and more rugged than I'd ever seen him.

"What are you all doing here?" I reached out to hold onto Charles for an anchor to keep me from floating away. He wrapped his arm around my shoulder and pulled me into his side.

"What nonsense!" grandmother snapped. "You are in trouble and we've come to help you. Did you think we wouldn't?"

"It's good to see you all," Charles said. "We're going to need your help. Minnie has been spotted on the Promenade, and we need everyone to take a different route there to try and track her down.

"Whatever you need, Beau," Joe said. And I remembered how they'd been good friends and probably still were. He must hate me for what I'd done to Charles. "Just tell us where you need us."

Charles began to give them all directions when my

phone rang again. Everyone stopped and looked at me.

Elisabeth. "Tell me you found her," I said into the phone.

"Duke found her."

Relief flooded me and I swayed on my feet. I nodded, to let everyone know they'd found her, but then I couldn't stop nodding. And I'd lost my words. Everyone blurred in front of me as tears welled up in my eyes.

Charles took the phone from my hand. "Elisabeth, April can't talk right now. Is Minnie okay?"

I clung to his shirt, to his warmth, and he held me up, pressing me to him.

"They're at the dog park by the river?" he said. "How did they get all the way over there? How did she even know to go there? That's where we go for Mickey's evening walk and she's never been th-- that dog."

"What? What is it?"

"Minnie didn't take Mickey for a walk. Mickey took her. He walked her all the way to his favorite park.

I'm going to send that dog away to obedience school until he learns to behave."

My legs crumpled and I slipped from Charles' arm to kneel on the sidewalk.

"April!" Everyone reached out to me in dismay, but I was…

Laughing.

I couldn't help myself. I was so panicked, so anxious, I had seriously been imagining the absolute worst case scenarios and all that had happened was that my wayward daughter and Charles' wayward dog had gone on an adventure like in some of her favorite books.

Suddenly Charles was right there with me on the sidewalk. "Are you alright, darling? We found her. She's okay."

"Yes, everything is alright. My life is a fairy tale. I have Minnie. I have my life. And somehow, for some reason, I've found my way back to you, as if by magic. It's a happy ending."

"We get to start over, April. We do." He looked at me as if nothing could be better than sitting with me on a Brooklyn sidewalk, laughing and crying together.

"We do," I said, and I hooked my arm around his neck and pulled him in so I could kiss him.

He smiled at me, and wiped the tears from my eyes after the kiss ended. "Should we go fetch our daughter and that damned dog?"

He stood and held his hand out to help me up, and I didn't let go as I faced my family.

"I guess the secret's out of the bag now," I said, too relieved to feel embarrassed. "I'm not a lesbian, I was never with Mona, and Charles is Minnie's father.

"You call him Charles?" Aunt Donna asked, a scandalized expression on her face.

"I do. I have ever since we were dating after Mom's wedding."

"Oh, the wedding," she said, and winked at Charles. "I told you, Beau."

"And I love him." I clung to his hand with both of mine.

"I love her, and I regret ever hiding our relationship from everyone so long ago. I'm not hiding anything anymore. We're together now, and still figuring out what that means, so would appreciate some space on the matter. But you'll have to excuse us. We're going to go get our daughter."

Jack, who had stood back and watched without comment until then stepped forward. "Let me drive you." His hair was much longer than I'd ever seen it, dark and curling over his ears.

Charles looked at Jacks' sports car and shook his head. "There's no room for us, Minnie and my dog in that car."

"You'll fit," Jack said.

"Nonsense, boys," Grandmother said, her cateye sunglasses gleaming, "Whittaker shall drive us. There's plenty of room in my car."

"Do you really want a dog in your car?" Jack asked.

"I want my great granddaughter in my car. Whittaker!" Her long suffering chauffeur opened the door for her while she gestured imperiously for us to follow.

There was nothing for it but to follow her.

Charles followed me and gave Whittaker the directions to the other dog park, and then I finally faced my grandmother.

"You look well, grandmother."

"Hmmph."

"I am glad to see you again."

"I don't appreciate leaving it to a crisis to finally get to see you."

"I'm sorry. I-- was afraid to come back. Afraid of the scandal I would cause."

"Scandal? You call an illegitimate child a scandal. In my day I knew a half dozen girls with that problem. They got married or they gave it away, they didn't run off into the wilds."

"Adirondacks, not the wilds."

"There is no appreciable difference, girl. Do you think I didn't have my own scandals? Do you think I didn't fancy inappropriate men?" She raised her chin and levelled a gaze at Charles. "And you, Mr Beau Beaumont. For shame on you. Letting her disappear on us and then not telling us that my namesake was your child."

"He didn't know, grandmother. He had nothing to do with it, don't blame him."

"Well he certainly had something to do with it!"

"I would marry her in a second, Minerva. I would have back then."

"And you right well should have. One doesn't go about impregnating girls of good family without being responsible for the results. And you are supposed to be a responsible fellow. Very bad form, Beau. I expect you to make up for it as soon as possible."

"And that's why I left! I refused to have my life planned out before I knew what I wanted, just so that I would avoid scandal. I wasn't going to force Charles to marry me. I couldn't do that to him. What did I care about a scandal? I was in love. And Minnie was born from love. I left so I could raise her in love."

Grandmother harrumphed and stomped her cane on the floorboards of the luxurious car. "You gave up the life to which you were born. Your fortune."

"I didn't need it. I didn't want it. I was happy."

"But you're back now, aren't you? It seems you weren't that happy. There were some things you were missing." She looked at Charles.

"It wasn't me. It was her friends, Mona and Elisabeth. They convinced her to come back to New York City."

Grandmother sat back, looking entirely too pleased with herself.

Looking entirely too suspicious.

"Wait. Why aren't you asking questions about them?" I did not trust my grandmother not to have her fingers in everything.

"Oh, I know about them. The vegetarian and the bisexual."

I turned to face her completely. "You didn't call her a lesbian."

"Well why would I? I know the difference between a lesbian and a bisexual. One limits herself to women, and the other has a wider range of romantic candidates."

"You've been talking to Mona."

"Moi?" She pressed a hand to her chest. "Of what do you accuse me?"

"Grandmother, did you have something to do with getting me to come back to New York?"

She put both hands on her cane and looked forward. "I saw a good investment opportunity with my step granddaughter, and I took it."

"Grandmother! Did you invest in the restaurant?"

"I bought the house."

"Because you wanted me to come home?"

"Because I wanted you to come back to the family and I wanted to meet my namesake and that Elisabeth has a brilliant plan for an empire of vegan restaurants all throughout the tri state area. This is just the beginning. The girl is a genius. Give her a chance and she'll take over the world."

"They've been working with you."

She lifted one shoulder in a nearly imperceptible shrug. "I am a woman who gets what she wants." The car pulled up to the dog park. "And I have many avenues to make sure it happens."

"Grandmother…" I didn't know how to respond and the words stuck in my throat. She had missed me and wanted me home. And she'd lured me back with friends and a place to make my art. Was I grateful or furious?

She waved her hand as if she didn't want any fuss. "I know you're an independent woman. My daughter has never been comfortable with that. She wants you to follow her rules, but you like to go on adventures yourself, like my namesake." She nodded out the window, where Minnie was playing with Mickey and Elisabeth. Happily. Duke was leaning against the fence outside of the dog park.

Then I really did get choked up and let out a sob.

"Go on, girl. Go get your child."

Whittaker came around and opened the door, holding out a hand to help me out, which was good, because I nearly tripped over myself trying to get to Minnie.

"Mama!" She saw me first. Her hair was straggling from her pigtails, but otherwise, she looked okay.

"Minnie, honey!" I ran to the gate, struggling with it. Charles was right behind me, unlatching the gate to let me in.

I swept Minnie up in my arms and she began to bawl. "Mama, I'm so sorry. I wanted to take Mickey for a walk and then I got lost and didn't know how to get back, so I followed him because I thought maybe he'd take me home like grandma's dogs do, but he just took me to the dog park, so I stayed here because I didn't know what else to do."

"It's okay, baby, it's okay." All my tears were gone, I could be strong for her and give her what she needed. I stroked her hair and held her to me. "You did the right thing staying in one place until we could find you."

I looked up to see Charles holding back, watching us. He had tears in his eyes, and he smiled at me, gratefully. I nodded him over. I wanted him with us. He deserved to be with us.

"Hey, Minnie," he said, tucking a strand of hair behind her ear. "We were really worried. Please don't wander off alone again."

She threw herself into his arms straight from mine and he held on for dear life. "I'm so sorry, Daddy. I thought if I had Mickey it didn't count as being alone. But he's not like a grown up at all. He's more like another kid. He just wanted to play. And he ate an icecream cone that someone dropped on the ground. Even though I told him no."

He laughed and then half sobbed. "Yes. I think you're the responsible one in this duo. Maybe you're the big kid and he's the little one even though he's huge and you're little."

Minnie laughed at the joke and Charles wiped his tears and laughed with her. He held her so strong and sure and I just knew he loved her and would never let her down. He would be the kind of father to her that my father never was. He would be the family that I needed. He was mine, and I loved him more than I ever realized.

My heart swelled looking at them. He'd stayed calm for me, supported me, but he'd been just as worried as I had. I took Lissie's handkerchief out of my pocket and handed it to him.

"I'm so glad our family is back together." I said, and then looked over at the car. "Speaking of, Minnie, there's someone else who'd like to meet you."

"Another brother?"

"Not this time, it's your great grandma."

"Oh, another grandma! Yay." She was ready for it, up for more.

"Actually, soon you'll get to meet a whole bunch of relatives. Another grandma and grandpa, a great aunt, and an uncle. Are you up to meeting them?"

"I have so much family!" Her eyes were wide and green and she blinked at me.

"They all came to meet you and make sure you were safe. They were worried about you."

"I'm fine now. Although I was so glad to see Duke on his motorcycle. And he called Lissie right away. Don't tell Lissie, but he gave me an ice cream cone, and that's not vegan. And maybe Mickey knocked it out of my hand and that's the one he ate off the ground."

"That dog needs to be trained." Charles grumbled.

"He certainly does," Grandmother said. "In the front seat with you, hound." Whittaker opened up the passenger side door and Mickey hopped in, looking not the least bit guilty.

Charles invited everyone back to his brownstone on the Promenade, since it was larger than my place, and he could have his housekeeper cook a luncheon for everyone.

I couldn't believe that my whole life had turned upside down and then righted itself again all before noon, but it had. I climbed into my grandmother's limo and settled Minnie on my lap.

He slid in next to me, and I rested my head on his shoulder, with my daughter in my arms.

"We get to have a happy ending," I whispered to him.

He kissed my temple. "Let yourself believe it, darling."

Minnie's birthday was a week later. Due to the sudden inclusion of a surprise family, the guest list had more than doubled. I offered to host the party at my brownstone, which was larger than April's apartment and where the garden served as a secret garden backdrop for the festivities. Between everyone, it was strung with paper lanterns and flowers and balloons in every color of the rainbow. Mrs. Edwards made sure to have plenty of the multi colored little cakes that Minnie loved, but also every food she could make in the color of the rainbow, including a lovely fruit salad, which was vegan.

Minnie adored her namesake Minerva, and Minerva adored her right back, ensconced as she was on a throne like chair under an umbrella, with her driver there to get her whatever she needed, Minnie asked for counsel from her great grandmother for every detail of the party, and together they ran the festivities like a pair of martinets.

Minnie's great aunt Donna ordered an ice sculpture in the shape of a goldendoodle, although her grandmother Barbara had tried to argue that ice sculptures were gauche. In the end, the little girls loved it and enjoyed posing for photos standing between the real Mickey and the Ice Mickey. Joe reminded Barbara that seven year old girl parties weren't supposed to be sophisticated and jollied her into taking some of the sparkling punch.

Barbara still hadn't forgiven Mona for stealing April away. She didn't quite believe that April had never been a lesbian, despite all evidence to the contrary. And because of that, April still held back from her mother, although she was happy to see the rest of her family again.

Jack surprised me by welcoming her back even more than anyone. I'd known that April hadn't had the best relationship with him, but he ran interference between Barbara and April, and I was glad for him. Surprisingly, he also ran interference between

Barbara and Mona, the despised lesbian who had stolen her away.

That was amusing, watching Jack trying to keep Mona busy on the other side of the room with Mona trying to shed him.

I sidled up to April, who looked lovely today, as she did every day, with her hair loose and flowing and her own rainbow colored cotton sundress in honor of Minnie's favorite colors. I kissed her cheek and pointed at the two of them. "Look at that, your brother and Mona are making friends."

She peered, doubtfully. "I don't think that's what that is. She hates him. She calls him Jackass. I think they're arguing."

I tried to see what she saw, but it looked to me like Jack was smiling and Mona was pretending she wasn't enjoying his attention. "Maybe they are," I said. "But those two are definitely not arguing."

I pointed at Duke, who had been given a special invitation as Minnie's rescuer, and Elisabeth. They were laughing and happy, and standing rather close together.

"You may be right. I wouldn't count on that lasting

though," she giggled and pulled my arm around her so she could snuggle. I was glad to oblige. "Everyone's happy. And that's good. It's nice just to be here in your arms.

"Ahh," I said. "You're right. Everyone is busy and happy. I have something I want to show you. Come with me."

"I can't leave, Charles. I'm hosting a party."

"Mrs Edwards is in charge of the food. Duke and Elisabeth are stationed at the drink table. Your grandmother is dictating the games and all the girls... look they've made her wear a fairy crown like all the other girls."

April smiled. "Oh, that's lovely."

I kissed her ear. "It is. So you should come with me."

April looked at me suspiciously, as she should, I definitely had something up my sleeve. But I smiled innocently and spread my hands. "Don't you trust me, darling?"

She frowned. "I do." She didn't say it with much enthusiasm, and I laughed.

I took her hand and drew her away, back into the

coolness of the house, through the kitchen and up the stairs.

"Where are you taking me Charles, we can't have sex now. It's Minnie's birthday party."

"You are so suspicious. It's not that."

I kept leading her up. Up past the second floor where my bedroom and office was, up past the third floor where Matthew lived when he was here.

"Charles…"

"I wanted you to see something I've never had the chance to show you in the delirious days we've been back together."

I led her up to the top of the house and opened the door out onto the roof deck.

It was one of the reasons I had bought this house, with the broad view of downtown Manhattan and the silvery water, and the sky arcing high above us.

"Oh! It's beautiful. It feels so free. What a lovely breeze."

"Do you like it? You can come here every day, you know."

"Charles…" she said, warning me. I was not supposed to push. And I knew it.

"I'm not asking you, yet. But I can try to make you want to live with me, can't I? That's not against the rules is it? To give you the opportunity to be happy?"

She rolled her eyes and stepped into me, pressing her body against mine. "There aren't any rules."

"Oh there aren't?"

"Of course not. We're just two people trying to figure out what this thing between us is. There are no rules."

"Ah." I put a finger to her chin so she'd look me in the eyes. "But I know what this is, darling. I've been around long enough to recognize that this, what is between us, is precious and rare." Her eyes were bright amber in the sun, her cheeks touched with a flush. "This is love, and it's forever."

"Charles…."

"We were apart for seven years, my love. Seven long years where nothing felt quite right, because you were gone. I need you in my life, April. I need you because we belong together."

She nodded and slipped her hands around my neck to pull me in for a kiss. This was what I needed. Her. Her lips, soft and sweet. Her warm embrace and silky skin. The floral essence of her hair. The eagerness with which her tongue met mine. "You're right," she murmured against my mouth. "This is love."

I reached into my pocket and took out the gift I had for her. No fanfare. No pronouncement, I didn't want to make a big deal. I simply unhooked her hands from around my neck and tucked it into her palm.

"What's this?" she asked as she stepped back, puzzled, opening her hand to see the antique art deco engagement ring that had been my great grandmother's. She gasped when she realized what it was, her startled eyes leaping to meet mine. "Are you serious? We said we were going to take this slow."

"Yes, I am serious. I'm serious about you. And I intend to marry you. But..." I reached into my other pocket and took out the other part of my gift. The gold chain slithered to hang from my fingers as I held it up for her. "I'm not asking you to marry me right now. That diamond ring is to show you my intentions, to make sure you understand how serious I am about you. But this chain, this is to show you my respect for you, for your boundaries and your concerns and your independence." I unlatched the chain and opened it up, taking the ring that was lax in her grip, and stringing the ring onto it. I dangled the ring up for her to see.

"I want to marry you. I love you. I love you as the mother of my child and we are now, always, no matter what you decide, a family, even if you choose to leave me again--"

"I wouldn't!" she gasped. "I promise."

"I believe you, but you still have the choice, and I want you to be able to choose of your own free will. I want you to know that I am yours, no matter what. But you are still free to choose your own life."

She looked for a moment like the air had left her body as her shoulders hunched and her face paled. "I can't-- I can't wear your ring on a chain!" She gasped raggedly, tears in her eyes. "I can't--" And then words failed her.

My heart sank to my feet. She didn't want to be with me. Her fear would always be between us. It was not something she could get over. "I'm sorry, I won't ask again," I said though the words did not want to leave my mouth and I felt deadened.

"No!" She cried.

"I'll give you some time alone." I turned to walk away, not able to face her anymore, needing that alone time myself as I processed her reluctance, her horror even at my proposal… not even a proposal, just a suggestion that maybe someday we might be together permanently.

Before I could go, she grabbed my hand and pulled me back. Crying. "No! Don't you dare!" Then she dropped to one knee in front of me. I reached to catch her but she just took my other hand too. "You idiot. I didn't mean that."

I was too confused and I didn't know how to respond anymore.

"You idiot," she repeated, this time more softly. "You idiot." She kissed my hand. "Oh my god, Charles, I love you. I can't imagine my life without you anymore. I need you so much. How could you think I wouldn't want to be with you?"

"I just wanted--"

"Shush," she said, pressing my palm to her cheek. "It's my turn to talk now."

"I'm sorry, please go ahead." Nothing else in the world was as important as what she said next.

"Charles, my love," she smiled up at me. "Will you marry me?"

I stared down at her, not sure I comprehended her. "Are you serious?"

She nodded, tears leaking from her eyes. "When you said I could make the choice to leave you, I suddenly realized that I couldn't ever make that choice. It would destroy me."

I got down on my knees to be on the same level as she was. I put my hand to her other cheek so I could hold her precious face. "Are you sure?"

"Yes, I'm sure. I've been afraid for so long of the worst thing that could happen in life, thinking that everything that happened would end in disaster, and then last week, it almost did, but you were there by my side every moment and you gave me faith and helped me find direction and stood behind me when I was weak, and gave me hope to carry on. You were how I came through that without going crazy. You made me believe. You gave me my happy ending. You are my happy ending. Charles Beau Beaumont, will you marry me? I will never be foolish again--

well I will be, but I'll listen to you when I am and get my sense back."

I kissed her and she laughed against my lips. I laughed with her. "Finally!" I said, breaking the chain as I pulled the ring from it. "Yes, April Hamilton, I will marry you." I slid the diamond onto her finger and she threw her arms around me, knocking us both to the floor... which was fine, since I had her on top of me and I liked it very much.

She began unbuttoning my shirt and I almost let her, before groaning and stopping her hand. "Darling, it's our daughter's seventh birthday party and I think we should save this for tonight, and maybe tell her that her mother and father are getting married."

She sighed, then climbed up off me, reaching a hand down to help me up. I didn't need the help but I liked holding her hand.

"Okay, let's go tell Minnie we get to keep her dad."

"You certainly do." I stole one more kiss and then we went down to break the news to our family.

ALSO BY L.A. PEPPER

Free copy of *Lovesick,* **A Best Friends Brother Secret Baby Romance**

https://dl.bookfunnel.com/tl5zurdlke

CONNECT WITH THE AUTHOR

L.A. Pepper's Author Page:
https://www.amazon.com/LA-
Pepper/e/B07QS4RJY6?
ref_=dbs_p_ebk_r00_abau_000000

Join L.A. Pepper's Private VIP Group here:
https://www.facebook.com/groups/3327853073170
33/?ref=bookmarks

Printed in Great Britain
by Amazon

18720519R00160